"I just couldn't go
Sunday night feel
I can't focus on w
I can't… You're in my head all the
time…."

"Yeah," Jani whispered. "You're causing me that same problem."

She couldn't tell whether that pleased him or not. But she didn't really care. She was too lost in looking at him, at that impressive collection of features and those penetrating iridescent sea-green eyes.

And there was something undeniable and irresistible happening at that moment between them that she just couldn't fight.

So when he came, Jani went slowly forward, too.

Dear Reader,

It's January Camden's turn up to bat. On behalf of her family, she must meet and get to know a man named Gideon Thatcher. The Thatcher family took a very big fall due to things done decades ago by Jani's great-grandfather, the founder of the Camden empire. A big fall that's left Gideon hating the Camdens.

Jani agrees that amends should be made to the people wronged in the building of the Camden Superstores, but she isn't enthusiastic about the timing on this. Due to being reproductively challenged, she needs to focus all her energies on becoming a mother ASAP.

And as determined as Jani is to have a baby, that's how determined Gideon is to never again let a child into his life. And to father Camden babies? Unthinkable!

So when a very hot attraction develops between the two of them, it puts them on a rocky road.

I hope you like bumpy rides!

Happy reading,

Victoria Pade

A BABY
IN THE BARGAIN

VICTORIA PADE

HARLEQUIN® SPECIAL EDITION®

Recycling programs
for this product may
not exist in your area.

ISBN-13: 978-0-373-65736-0

A BABY IN THE BARGAIN

Printed in U.S.A.

Books by Victoria Pade

VICTORIA PADE

is a *USA TODAY* bestselling author of numerous romance novels. She has two beautiful and talented daughters—Cori and Erin—and is a native of Colorado, where she lives and writes. A devoted chocolate lover, she's in search of the perfect chocolate-chip-cookie recipe. For information about her latest and upcoming releases, and to find recipes for some of the decadent desserts her characters enjoy, log on to www.vikkipade.com.

Chapter One

Two hours and twenty-three minutes. That was how long January Camden had been waiting in her car on that Monday afternoon. Actually, it was Monday evening by then because it was now twenty-three minutes after six o'clock. And she decided that, for her, there was no appeal to being a stalker.

But stalking Gideon Thatcher at his place of business was what she'd been reduced to.

She closed the book she'd been reading when it was still light out, put it into her oversize hobo purse and turned on the engine of her sedan in order to run the heat for a few minutes.

It was the end of January—the month of her birth and the reason for her name. And although the daytime weather in Denver had been unseasonably warm and springlike, it was now after dark and getting much colder, forcing her to start her car and turn on the heater more frequently than when she'd first begun this quest today.

How late did this guy work, anyway?

She knew that Gideon Thatcher was in the office because she'd called and quizzed the receptionist before beginning this stakeout. The helpful older-sounding woman had said that he was expected to be there until five.

Jani had arrived in the heart of downtown Denver at four o'clock. She'd taken one turn around the block to make sure there wasn't a rear exit to the redbrick turn-of-the-century mansion that had been remodeled into office space. Then she'd parked on the street two car lengths from the front of the building where she could see the entrance.

At that point she'd placed a second call to the Thatcher Group's receptionist and again asked if Gideon Thatcher was in. *"In, but not available"* had been the answer. So she'd been waiting ever since to ambush the man. She'd seen pictures of him on his website and in a recent newspaper article, so she was certain that he hadn't slipped by without her recognizing him.

Gideon Thatcher was the owner of the Thatcher Group, a private company that offered city planning services. The article had brought him to Jani's grandmother's immediate attention, leading seventy-five-year-old Georgianna Camden to recruit Jani for her project of making amends to the victims of the Camden family's past business misdeeds.

The Camdens owned Camden Incorporated, which encompassed a worldwide chain of superstores and many of the factories, warehouses, production facilities, ranches and farms that stocked them. An empire. Built by Jani's great-grandfather, H. J. Camden.

The caring family man she'd loved.

Unfortunately, when it had come to business, H. J. Camden had been very different from the way he'd been at home. It had always been rumored that he was ruthless, that he had trampled and sacrificed numerous people in the building of the Camden empire. That he'd instilled this ruthlessness in his son, Hank, and even in his grandsons—Jani's late father, Howard, and her uncle Mitchum.

The family had hoped the rumors weren't true. It just didn't sound like the kind, loving men whom Jani, her siblings and her cousins had experienced. But now, thanks to finding H.J.'s journals, the worst of the stories about his business dealings had been confirmed.

And so Georgianna had drafted H.J.'s ten descendants, sending them on fact-finding missions to learn how best to make some sort of compensation to his victims and their families. They were determined to do what they could to atone to some of the people most wronged in the past.

But Gideon Thatcher wasn't making this easy for Jani. He'd denied her request for a meeting with him. He hadn't answered her voice mails or emails or the letter she'd sent to him. She wasn't sure what else to do but lie in wait for him and try to force him to talk to her. Essentially she was stalking him.

Jani sat up straight and arched away from the car seat to ease the kink out of her back, then slipped her arms into the navy blue wool peacoat she'd taken off when it was warmer. She buttoned it over her white turtleneck sweater and navy wool slacks.

"Come on, just quit for the day and go home," she said, staring in the direction of the front door where other people had already emerged in end-of-the-work-day mode.

But nothing happened at her command. Bored and antsy, she took a lip gloss from her purse and craned up to her rearview mirror to apply it.

She'd always wished that her mouth wasn't quite as wide as it was, and the rectangular mirror only seemed to accentuate that flaw. She puckered up a little just to make herself feel better. Then, when she'd applied the lip gloss, she took stock of the rest of what she could see in the small reflection.

No mascara smudges to muddy her blue eyes—the blue eyes that all ten of Georgianna's grandchildren had and that had, over the years in school, come to be known as the Camden blue eyes.

Her high cheekbones still bore the pink blush she'd applied that morning when she'd left her house but she reached into her purse to retrieve her compact so she could blot her straight forehead, her nose and the chin that was a tiny bit on the pointy side.

Then she moved her head this way and that to get a glimpse of her hair in the sliver of mirror.

The thick, wavy, sable-colored locks seemed a little scraggly so she put the compact back in her purse and took out a brush.

Ordinarily she would have tilted her head upside down to brush her hair from the bottom up but since that wasn't possible in the car, she ran the brush through from the top to the ends that fell six inches below her shoulders. Then she shook her head to get her hair to fall slightly forward.

It was something she'd been doing since the sixth grade when Larry Driskel had remarked that her nose was long and skinny. Her grandmother complained that her hair was *in* her face and always said that she was too pretty to hide behind it. But, since Larry Driskel's comment, Jani just felt more confident with her hair acting as a bit of a curtain between her and the world.

And the thought of Gideon Thatcher definitely left her with the need to feel as confident as possible—it was unnerving to have to meet someone for the first time who potentially didn't like the Camdens. And forcing that meeting didn't help.

Of course it was possible that she was just misinterpreting why Gideon Thatcher had rejected her every overture. That's what her more optimistic side told her. Maybe he was just a busy guy and didn't have the time for her. Maybe what H.J. had done years and years ago to Gideon Thatcher's family wasn't any big deal to him....

Jani hoped that was the case but not even her optimistic side really believed it.

She took a deep breath and turned off her engine, thinking that she would wait until seven. If Gideon Thatcher didn't come out by then, she'd go up to the office and just barge in.

But about the time she reached that decision, the large mahogany front door to the building opened and out stepped the man himself.

Jani recognized him from his photos but instantly realized that none of them had done him justice.

Which was why she uttered an involuntary "Wow…" and just sat there staring.

Gideon Thatcher was tall, commanding and broad-shouldered in a black overcoat and carrying a leather briefcase. Even from a distance she could see that he was remarkably good-looking.

The glow of the streetlights illuminated brown hair a couple of shades lighter than hers—a sandy, golden brown. He wore it short on the sides, slightly longer on top and carelessly combed. And although Jani was too far away to analyze each of his features, he was just so generally handsome that it was enough to make her jaw drop a little.

While she sat there stunned, he seemed to remember something, then turned and disappeared back into the building.

That was actually a lucky break, Jani thought. Because she should have already made her approach but there she was, still sitting in her car, dumbstruck by the sight of him.

Gambling that he would come out again any minute, Jani took her keys from the ignition and grabbed her purse. She hurried out of her sedan, closed the door and went to the foot of the seven stone steps that rose to the former mansion's front door.

Which was when that door opened again and out came Gideon Thatcher for the second time.

"Mr. Thatcher?" she said brightly.

The sound of her voice brought him to a stop. They'd never met so of course he didn't recognize her; he merely looked at her quizzically. But after a split-second appraisal he smiled a reserved smile that kept his fairly full lips closed but turned up the corners of his mouth. His finely shaped eyebrows arched in interest. A flattering kind of interest that Jani hadn't seen from a man in a while so it set off a little rush of satisfaction. Particularly when that interest was coming from someone this handsome.

He had a wide forehead; penetrating eyes she still couldn't see the color of; a nose that was just long enough and just wide enough to suit his face; and a jawline that was well angled, chiseled and culminated in a squared-off chin that had a dashing off-center dent in it.

But she was gawking again...

"I'm Gideon Thatcher," he confirmed as he came down the steps without touching the wrought-iron railing on either side of them.

Standing before her, he was at least eight inches taller than her five-foot-four height and now she could see that his eyes were green. An almost iridescent sea green, and gorgeous.

"I'm January Camden—"

Whoops. That was all it took to alter things.

Gideon Thatcher's gorgeous green eyes narrowed at her, and his attractive face not only sobered, but went instantly hostile.

Jani pretended not to notice. "I've been trying to speak with you—"

"I don't know why you're here and I don't care," he announced unceremoniously in his deep voice. "I have nothing to say to any Camden, anytime, anywhere."

Okay, not a warm reception.

What did you get me into, GiGi? she silently asked of her grandmother.

But within the Camden organization, Jani was in charge of public relations and marketing. Part of her job was to not get ruffled in the face of irate customers, vendors, clients and anyone else she needed to deal with. She had no idea why something about Gideon

Thatcher *was* ruffling her a little on the inside but she hid it.

"If you could just give me a few minutes—"

"No matter what you Camdens have up your sleeve, I'm not interested. Regardless of how pretty a package they've sent to tempt me with."

It took Jani a split second to realize that he was talking about her. Giving her a sort of compliment.

The problem was, in that instant of confusion, Gideon Thatcher stepped around her and was headed on his way.

"Please, if you could just give me a minute..." she beseeched, turning quickly to follow him.

Unfortunately when she did that, the strap on her purse caught on the end of the stair railing and broke. Her purse fell, spewing the contents across the sidewalk and even under the car parked at the curb, eliciting a loud gasp from Jani.

Gideon Thatcher paused and looked back.

As Jani began to gather her spilled belongings she could see enough peripherally to tell that he was aggravated. But rather than continuing on his way and leaving her to the mess, he muttered something under his breath and returned to help her pick things up.

While Jani snatched her wallet, cell phone and some other personal items, he went to the curb and leaned far over to reach what had slid under the car.

So You Want to Have a Baby—that was the name of the book she'd been reading while she waited for him. The title was in big black block letters that had jumped out at her at the bookstore. His gaze went to the cover, no doubt registering the title, as he handed the book to her.

Jani accepted the book, and quickly stuffed it into her purse. Then he gave her the compact and a tablet she'd been taking notes on as she'd read.

"Thank you," she said, fighting the embarrassment of having him know what she was reading.

But she wasn't about to address the topic with him and instead decided that the delay her spilled purse had caused was an opportunity she couldn't let pass. It was as if fate had given her another chance to say what she'd come to say in the first place.

So she did. "We saw the article in the paper about all you're doing to redevelop Lakeview and we want to fund a park in your great-grandfather's name."

A stillness seemed to come over Gideon Thatcher as he stared at her in disbelief. Then he shook his handsome head, and made a sort of huffing sound, practically scoffed at her.

"H. J. Camden used and betrayed my great-grandfather, and made it look as if my great-grandfather betrayed hundreds of people who trusted him," Gideon Thatcher proclaimed. "He ruined the Thatcher name and turned Lakeview into something it never wanted to be. You have no idea what I had to do to convince Lakeview to give me—a *Thatcher*—this project. And now you not only think that I would let the Camdens anywhere near it, but you have the gall to believe that something as meager as a *park* would somehow make up for everything?"

"H.J. and your great-grandfather were good friends for fifteen years. I know things went bad but in some respects it wasn't H.J.'s fault—he wanted to keep the promises he made—"

"*I'm* keeping the promises he made. H. J. Camden didn't do anything for anyone but himself."

Jani couldn't deny that. And, as she stood there facing Gideon Thatcher's scorn and contempt, she had to wonder if anything she offered would break through it.

But the family had vowed to explore all the ramifications of H.J.'s actions and in order to do that she had to get her foot in the door with this guy.

So she stood her ground, raised her chin proudly and said, "If not a park, then what?"

"You're kidding, right? You think that anything—*anything*—can make up for what H. J. Camden did to my family?"

"I think that you see this only from your own perspective right now and that other factors went into what happened decades ago. But H.J.—*my* great-grandfather—regretted how things ended up. He regretted the loss of his friendship with your great-grandfather. He regretted that Lakeview was left a factory and warehouse town rather than the suburban dream he promised. And now that it seems as if you're going to do so much of what should have been done then, we know that H.J. would want your great-grandfather honored by helping in some way."

"Some token way—like a measly park?"

A park or whatever, Jani thought. She just needed to make enough of a connection with this man to get to know him, find out what actually happened to his family post-H.J. and learn if there were any other ways the Camdens could make up for the past.

"You were quoted in the newspaper saying something about a park in Lakeview," she continued. "That's the only reason we're suggesting that. If there's something else that we could do, something that you would rather have the Thatcher name on, we could certainly talk about it."

"We could, could we?" he said sarcastically. "The high-and-mighty Camdens would *allow* that?"

She hadn't said it that way and she certainly hadn't meant it that way.

"Mr. Thatcher…" she said, hoping that calling him that would show her respect.

But that was as far as she got.

"Gideon," he corrected as if she were insulting him in some way to use the formality, and Jani realized that she couldn't win.

"Gideon," she amended patiently. "We just want to do what we can to help Lakeview finally become what it should have, and we want to do it in the name of your great-grandfather."

"It sure as hell wouldn't be in the name of Camden."

"Whatever we do can be absolutely anonymous. We aren't looking for any kind of credit—"

"And you aren't going to get any."

Oh, he really did have a grudge against them. It seemed as if the mission to makes amends had been so much simpler for her brother Cade, who had ended up meeting the love of his life when he'd accomplished the first of these tasks a few months ago.

But rather than a repeat of that scenario, here Jani was, standing on a downtown Denver street being glared at by a man incited to fury by the mention of her family name. And she had something that was so much more important to her that she *wanted* to be putting her time and energy into. That she *needed* to be putting her time and energy into.

But she, like the rest of her siblings and cousins, was devoted to the grandmother who had raised them all. And since Georgianna had asked that they each accept whichever of these undertakings she assigned them, Jani was stuck. She had to make the best of this.

"We don't want credit," she assured him, "we only want to contribute in any way that you see fit to honor your great-grandfather."

Gideon Thatcher went on staring at her, studying her as if he were trying to see through to the truth he seemed to think was behind what she was saying.

But there was nothing for him to see through because what Jani had said *was* the truth.

"Please. If you'd just think about it. It can be on your terms…" she told him in all honesty.

"My terms…" he echoed.

"Absolutely."

His eyes narrowed even more at her, and she knew he wasn't convinced.

But maybe something he saw in her helped a little because after what seemed like an interminable pause, he actually conceded. "I'll think about it."

Jani thought that was as good as it was going to get at that point, and she jumped on it.

She rummaged in the jumble of her purse until she found a pen and the small case that held her business cards. When she had them in hand, she wrote her cell phone number and her home phone number on the back of the card—wondering even as she did if he really needed her home phone number, yet inclined to give it to him anyway.

Not for any personal reason, she told herself. Only to make sure he knew that she meant everything she'd said and wanted to be accommodating. Whether he was a great-looking guy or not, she wouldn't want to get involved with someone predisposed to despising her even if she had the time to spend on that. Which she didn't.

When she finished jotting on the back of the card, she handed it to him. "These are all the numbers where I can be reached—day or night, whatever is convenient for you..."

Gideon Thatcher glanced at the card he held in a hand that was big and strong-looking—somehow one of the sexiest hands Jani had ever taken notice of. Although she wasn't quite sure what constituted a sexy hand...

"January Camden," he read out loud.

"Jani—you can call me Jani. My friends and family do."

He raised those iridescent green eyes to her again and while the hostility was gone from his expression, what had replaced it was something that let her know that if he took her up on her offer he would make it a challenge for her.

Then he confirmed her hunch by saying, "You're going to be sorry that you approached me today, *January.* If I decide to take your guilty-conscience money it'll be for a lot more than a park. In the name of Franklin Thatcher and the community of Lakeview, I'll make sure your bottom line feels some pain."

Jani held her head high. "We're serious about wanting to honor your great-grandfather in whatever way you think best. I hope you'll be in touch soon."

"Soon enough," he said ominously.

Jani wasn't sure how to respond to that. But since he was still standing there staring at her she thought that it was up to her to bring this meeting to a conclusion, so she said, "I'll let you get on your way, then. I'm parked right over there..."

He glanced at the car she'd indicated then back at her, and it crossed her mind to offer a parting handshake the way she might at the end of a business meeting.

But the moment the thought flitted through her brain she realized that she liked the idea of making physical contact with him a little too much. That something in her was overly eager to experience the feel of that hand she'd found sexy.

It was weird. And she didn't think it was wise to give in to it.

So she merely said a perfunctory, "Thanks for your time."

"Uh-huh" was his only answer.

He continued to stand there and Jani realized that, in the same way he'd helped with her spilled purse, he might be begrudgingly offering her the courtesy of making sure she got safely to her car. So that was where she headed.

It was unsettling, though, to have his gaze remain on her while she rummaged a third time in her purse for her car keys, unlocked her door and got behind the wheel.

More unsettling still when she started the engine and cast a glance out the passenger window to see that Gideon Thatcher had gone on watching her even now that she was safely locked in.

Didn't he trust her to keep her word enough to drive away? Because suspicion was clearly in his expression, as if he were wondering what exactly she was up to.

Don't worry, I'm a good person...

And she wanted him to know that.

In fact it surprised her to discover how much she wanted him to know that.

Almost as much as she wished that the way he'd looked at her before he'd heard her name had been the way he'd kept looking at her.

But none of that was important, she told herself. She had a job to do for the family and that was all this was. And when it was over she would get on with her plans to have a baby and that would be that for Gideon Thatcher.

Yet as she finally pulled out into a break in traffic and saw him turn and head in the opposite direction down the sidewalk, she felt the tiniest twinge of regret that a man like that disliked her so much just because of who she was.

A man like that...

It would be nice if a man like that had an entirely different response to her.

Nice if there had been a man like that in her life a while ago, when she could have started and built a relationship.

Because, oh, she and a man like that could have made wonderful babies together...

Silly, silly thought...

And it only popped into her head, she told herself, because she had making babies on the brain these days.

Not because of Gideon Thatcher in particular.

Even though he was a man like that...

Chapter Two

"You're late."

"Sorry," Gideon said to Jack Durnham, his best friend and second-in-command of the Thatcher Group. "Bad night. Too many things rolling around in my head. I didn't fall asleep until about four this morning, and then I slept through the alarm. Maybe the boss won't notice if we sneak into the office with our coats over our heads."

"Good plan, boss," Jack said with a laugh.

The two had been friends since middle school. They'd gone to college together, been each other's best man at their weddings, and Jack had quit a lucrative job with a local engineering firm to come on board when Gideon had started the Thatcher Group. Technically Gideon was Jack's boss but Gideon saw him more as a partner than an employee.

"What was rolling around in your head to keep you up?" Jack asked after they'd ordered.

"You won't believe it when I tell you. But you first— how did your weekend with Sammy go?"

Jack grimaced and shook his blond head.

Sammy was his two-year-old son. Jack and his wife were recently separated and the three previous days were the first time Jack had had visitation with the toddler.

"Not great," Jack said. "Tiffany is making everything as difficult as possible. I don't know why—she's the one who decided our marriage was stagnating and wanted out. But for some reason I get to be punished. After the seven weeks in Florida with her parents that kept me from seeing Sammy at all, she came back to Colorado Springs rather than Denver. It's blackmail—if I want Sammy closer, I'll have to pay for a place for her to live here. Otherwise, it's an hour drive to the Springs to pick him up and an hour drive back to Denver to have him for the weekend. Then two more hours in the car for the return at the end of the visitation."

Jack's voice had gotten louder and angrier. Gideon could see that he needed to vent so he didn't point out that this was the same thing Jack had ranted about in advance of the three-day weekend he'd taken with his son.

"How about the visit itself? How did that go?" Gideon asked.

"I know how you ended up over Jillie. So you probably think that I should just count myself lucky that I get to see Sammy at all. But, dammit, this is so lousy! Sammy is two! He took one look at me after so long apart, latched onto Tiffany's leg and acted like I was a stranger. He cried when I took him, then glared at me the whole drive back to Denver. And to make things worse, once we got here and I needed to put him to bed, Tiffany hadn't packed that blanket thing he sleeps with—"

"Oh, that's bad!" Gideon commiserated. "Whatever it is they need to have with them when they go to sleep, they *need* to have."

"Right. I had to load him back into the car—tired, crabby and hating me for taking him away from his mother—and go to three different Camden Superstores to try to find a blanket thing exactly like the one he has. Luckily I did, but by then he was overwrought, and he just kept crying for Tiffany and—"

"You were both miserable."

"We were just getting back into the swing of things with each other by yesterday and I had to turn around and take him back," Jack concluded.

"You're right—that is lousy."

"I'm sorry," Jack apologized in a voice an octave lower than the one he'd been using. "Again, I know I'm better off than you are, but it still stinks."

"Yeah, it does," Gideon agreed. He could see clearly how much his friend was suffering and knew the feeling well. Too well. It served as a reminder of the reason for the decision he'd made for himself. The vow.

Their breakfasts arrived, and when the waitress had left Jack changed the subject.

"Okay, you know if you let me I'll gripe about this all day. Now tell me what was rolling around in your head to keep you up last night."

"Speaking of Camden Superstores…" Gideon said sarcastically, referring to his friend's mention of them.

"I know how you feel about the Camdens, but sometimes we all have to use the stores that made them rich. Even you."

Gideon avoided them but Jack was right, sometimes, in a pinch, he gave in and went into one of them.

"But how do we feel about taking Camden money for the Lakeview project…" he said.

Jack's forkful of eggs stalled midair. "Huh?"

"When I came out of work last night there was a hot little number waiting for me on the sidewalk—January Camden. I've had some messages from her but I've been ignoring them. Apparently the Camdens want to make a donation to fund a park in Lakeview, in my great-grandfather's name. They want to *honor* him."

"Guilty-conscience money?" Jack guessed.

"That's what I said."

"So, I know the story…" Jack mused as if he were updating himself. "H. J. Camden was friends with your great-grandfather and your great-grandfather was Lakeview's mayor, right? Back when Lakeview was a dying-out farm community with good proximity to Denver, Camden wanted to build warehouses and factories there. But Lakeview didn't want to be turned into a warehouse and factory district, so Camden sweetened the deal—he said if he could build what he wanted there, he'd spearhead the development of Lakeview into a post-war suburban dream. New homes, the coming of big and small businesses, schools and parks—"

"And he got my great-grandfather to support his plan," Gideon said. "He needed somebody who was well respected to go to bat for him. He needed influence with the city council—"

"Which—as mayor—your great-grandfather had."

"And trusting their mayor, Lakeview signed on—they gave Camden the okay for the factories and warehouses."

"But that was it for Camden," Jack said. "Once he had what he wanted, he didn't come through on the rest."

"And my great-grandfather got the blame."

"Along with all the retribution and the hardship that came with it and sifted down to your grandfather and your father and, ultimately, left you with things to deal with…" Jack nodded now that he knew they were on the same page. "You have good reason to feel the way you do about the Camdens. So what were you up all night doing? Thinking of ways to get even with them?"

"More like rehashing all the reasons I have for hating them. Fuming," Gideon said, not telling his friend that he'd needed to focus on the anger because otherwise his mind kept wandering back to January Camden.

The first thing he'd noticed was all that espresso-colored hair bathed in golden streetlight, falling in waves well past her shoulders like a dark frame around skin as flawless and pure as fresh cream—that image had flashed through his mind and defused some of the fuming.

And so had recollections of high cheekbones and that thin, perfectly shaped nose that was just long enough to lend a hint of the exotic to her face. Of those full lips, lush and lovely and way, way too kissable-looking. Of eyes so blue—so intensely, brightly, blueberry-blue—that he'd been bowled over by them by the time he'd reached the fourth step down from his office…

And here he was again, lost in the memory of the memory that had kept him up last night.

He shook his head. "Anyway, no, I wasn't thinking about getting even with them—it's not like I'm obsessed with them, or with payback or something. But it also isn't as if I want to get in bed with them, either..."

Where had that particular turn of phrase come from? And why had the picture of January Camden popped back into his brain along with it?

It's a figure of speech and that's all *it is,* he insisted to himself. *It doesn't have any hidden meaning.*

Still he found himself feeling a few degrees warmer all of a sudden and fidgeting in his chair a little to evade the involuntary response that was going through him.

"I know you wouldn't ever 'get into bed' with the Camdens," Jack said. "But would that be what a donation from them was?"

"I don't know," Gideon said with a sigh. "I do like the idea of putting my great-grandfather's name on something of value and service to Lakeview. And the Camdens sure as hell owe Lakeview."

"So you'd be killing two birds with one stone?"

"Except that the stone belongs to the Camdens, and they can't be trusted—my family history proves that," Gideon added, showing just how much he was vacillating about this.

"Do you think it's a trick of some kind?" Jack asked, as he finished with his breakfast and settled in with his second cup of coffee.

"I know I won't let it be. And she said that I can set the terms."

"So maybe this is on the up-and-up?" Jack suggested. "Maybe they really do just want to make up for what H.J. did?"

Gideon shrugged, showing his reservations.

"The Camdens *are* heavy into charity and benefits and good deeds now," Jack pointed out. "Hospital wings, libraries, research labs, animal shelters. They've even made donations huge enough to be newsworthy in national and international disasters. Their name crops up with just about anything worthwhile that goes on these days. Could it be that this is a generation of new-and-improved Camdens?"

"New-and-improved Camdens?" Gideon parroted. "I might not be looking to get even but I also don't know that I buy that, either. Don't forget that H.J. came into Lakeview a wolf in sheep's clothing."

"True. But your eyes are wide open when it comes to these people. And if their donation benefits a community they owe plenty to and your great-grandfather gets paid a little homage in the process, aren't those two good things?"

"I'm thinking about it," Gideon said evasively.

The waitress came to find out if they wanted anything. Jack took a refill on his coffee. Gideon just asked for the check.

"This is on me for keeping you waiting," he told his friend. "But I'm gonna have to leave you while you finish your coffee—I need to get to that meeting with Lakeview Parks and Recreation."

"Oh, right, I forgot about that. I'll see you at the office when you get back."

As Gideon fished in his wallet to leave the money for the check and a generous tip he said, "Don't worry about things with Sammy. This is the roughest time. He's still your son and you have every right to him, so it'll work out."

"Yeah," Jack said glumly. "But it'll never be the same."

Gideon couldn't refute that because he knew it was true. So he didn't try.

He merely said he'd see Jack later and left, knowing what his friend was going through and feeling a wave of old pain himself at the thought.

That pain lasted until he got behind the wheel of his SUV and headed for Lakeview. The thought of Lakeview brought January Camden and what she'd proposed back to mind to distract him.

If he decided to take her up on her offer and had to have contact with a Camden, at least it would be with a Camden who was easy on the eyes.

She'd been some kind of liaison to send. A real attention-getter. He had to give them credit for that, at least.

And she'd weathered the storm he'd sent her way with composure—she got points for that. Dignity and composure. And style—she had that, too. Dignity, composure, style, beauty…

Okay, yes, January Camden was something, he admitted reluctantly.

But she was still a Camden.

And even though he didn't remember seeing a wedding ring, she must be a married Camden. If that book that had fallen out of her purse was any indication, she was in starting-a-family mode.

The old pain swung back and hit him when that thought went through his head. Family. Babies. Kids…

And suddenly it wasn't January Camden he was picturing but the little girl who had been his own daughter. If only for a while…

Jillie.

His little Jillie-bean…

All this time and it could still knock him as cold as a fist to the jaw...

And it occurred to him that he'd actually *rather* think about January Camden than about Jillie. About all the Camdens. He'd rather be mad than maudlin and depressed....

So think about the donation...he told himself.

But *only* about the donation and the lousy, stinking, underhanded Camdens.

Not about the way January Camden looked or carried herself.

Not about her blue, blue eyes.

Not about what might be going on in her personal life.

Just the donation the lousy, stinking, underhanded Camdens wanted to make to Lakeview.

And whether or not he was going to let it happen...

"Aren't you guys having lunch with GiGi and me?" Jani asked Margaret and Louie, referring to Georgianna Camden by the nickname everyone used for her. Jani had come to her grandmother's house hoping for time alone with GiGi. But Margaret and Louie Haliburton were more than GiGi's house staff; they were the adopted members of the family who had helped GiGi raise her ten grandchildren. They continued to work and live on the estate, and to be important to GiGi and to all of the Camdens.

Because they were in the kitchen with GiGi when Jani arrived, she'd expected them to be staying for lunch, which meant she'd have to have a few words with her grandmother in private later. But after they'd all exchanged pleasantries, Louie announced that he and Margaret should be going.

"I'm being taken out to lunch," Margaret said with delight on her lined face. "I'd say Louie was becoming a romantic in his old age but I think you're grandmother put him up to it since he forgot our anniversary."

"Nah! It was my idea," Louie insisted.

"Better make it a long lunch, Louie, with a shopping spree afterward, or you're never getting out of the doghouse," GiGi advised him, laughing.

The camaraderie among the three older people was obvious. They were genuinely close friends and indispensable to each other.

"Yes, shopping—that's a good idea," Margaret said, although Jani wondered why it would appeal to the woman who mainly wore elastic-waistband slacks and either T-shirts or sweatshirts that always had messages printed on them.

Regardless, the couple said goodbye and went on their way, leaving Jani alone with her grandmother to sit at the breakfast nook that was large enough for fourteen people.

GiGi had made her special grilled-cheese sandwiches and tomato-basil soup. That was what they talked about as they began to eat.

But then Jani heard the sound of the front door closing, telling her that Margaret and Louie had left, so she moved on to the subject she'd come to discuss. The subject that was absolutely not to be shared outside the circle of the grandchildren and GiGi. Not even with Margaret and Louie.

Whatever misdeeds H. J. Camden had perpetuated, the family knew it was imperative to keep it quiet.

Prominence and wealth made them targets, and they didn't want to invite trouble.

"So I told you on the phone that I finally spoke to Gideon Thatcher," Jani said.

"How did it go?" the elderly woman inquired.

"Not well. He *hates* us, GiGi," Jani said, wasting no time getting to the point. "Decades and two generations between when H.J.'s promises to Lakeview fizzled out and now haven't made it any better—this guy hates us as much as if *he* was the one H.J. used to get those warehouses and factories built."

"Well, we *are* seeking out folks who got the short end of the stick from H.J.," GiGi said calmly.

"But maybe I'm not the best one to deal with it right now, when I've started with the infertility endocrinologist and the wheels are finally in motion for a baby."

Jani could see from the expression on Georgianna's face—which still showed glimmers of her early beauty—that her grandmother was trying to contain her disapproval of the course Jani had set for herself.

"You've made it clear that that's what you're going to do come hell or high water but I still don't agree with the rush," GiGi said bluntly. "I know when you had that appendectomy at seventeen and they found out you have only one ovary—"

"One unusually *small* ovary," Jani reminded. "Which means that from the get-go my chances for having a family are greatly reduced—you and I were both told that."

"I know that since then you've been scared silly that you wouldn't be able to have a baby at all."

"Because they made it clear there were risks, especially if I waited too long. 'The earlier the better'—that's what they said. And now I've turned *thirty! Thirty* and with all those years wasted on Reggie. I can't wait any longer, GiGi!"

"Eat some grilled cheese, tell me if there's enough garlic in the mayo," her grandmother advised.

Jani knew that was a diversion to keep her from getting too agitated. But it was difficult *not* to get agitated over this. Until now she'd followed the traditional route—she'd tried to find the right guy, get married, *then* have a family. The route her grandmother approved of.

But that route had led to a dead end and cost her precious time. Time she certainly didn't have to waste.

So she wasn't going to. She'd come to the firm conclusion that she had to bypass the step of finding another man to have a relationship with. She couldn't afford the months, the years that a relationship required to blossom, to develop. She couldn't afford the time it took to get to an engagement, a marriage. To only *then* pursue a pregnancy and have a baby. More years could be spent on that course.

Instead she'd decided to have a baby on her own. Here and now, without a husband. That's what she'd made up her mind to do. And that was what she was going to do. Despite the fact that to seventy-five-year-old Georgianna it wasn't merely unconventional, but bordered on scandalous.

"I'm just saying," Jani reasoned, getting back to her initial point, "that maybe it would be better to give this particular deal with Gideon Thatcher to someone else because so much of my energy will be devoted to getting pregnant."

Hmm… But why did the thought of her grandmother

giving this job to one of her female cousins make her feel a little jealous, a little territorial?

Jani didn't understand it.

But it was that feeling that prompted her to add, "Maybe one of the boys would be better…"

GiGi shook her head as she took a bite of her own sandwich. "I'm looking at it this way—let's say you *do* get pregnant—"

"I *will* get pregnant. I *have* to. It's my last chance."

GiGi humored her. "Yes, well. Once you do, then you'll *be* pregnant and dealing with that without even a husband to take care of you or help you—*that* wouldn't be a time to send you out on one of these missions, would it? Then you'll have a baby—on your own," the elderly woman emphasized. "I won't be able to ask you to leave a baby in order to spend time getting to know one of these people to find out how much damage was done and how we can make up for it, will I?"

GiGi had always been sharp as a tack and that hadn't changed with age. She'd also always been a step ahead of all ten of her grandchildren, and Jani could see that was still the case. Apparently GiGi had anticipated her arguments and prepared her rebuttal.

"So now is the *best* time for you to do this. Maybe the *only* time you'll be able to do it," GiGi concluded.

Jani had to laugh a little at her own defeat. Her grandmother was right—once she was pregnant and had a baby, she wasn't going to be in any position to do something like this. So rather than continue to fight it, she supposed she might as well concede.

At least, she told herself, GiGi wasn't trying to talk her out of having a baby on her own anymore, even if the elderly woman didn't like the idea.

Jani just hoped her grandmother didn't think that this project with Gideon Thatcher would keep her from pursuing the baby issue. Because she wouldn't let that—or anything else—get in her way. She would just schedule her appointments with the infertility doctor around whatever she had to do with the oh-so-good-looking man who saw her as the enemy. She wasn't going to cancel or postpone anything.

"Okay, you win," Jani said over a spoonful of the soup. "But this Thatcher guy isn't going to settle for only a park in his great-grandfather's name. He threw that back in my face. If he agrees to let us do something, it's going to have to be bigger. Probably a lot bigger."

GiGi shrugged. "Fine. Do whatever it takes to find out how much damage H.J. did, and if we can do more for the Thatchers themselves to make it up to them. Whatever he wants."

"What he wants is a Camden head on a platter."

GiGi slid out of the breakfast nook with her empty water glass in one hand. As she passed by the side of the nook where Jani was sitting, she took Jani's chin in her free hand, and tipped Jani's face upward for close scrutiny the way she had when Jani was just a little girl.

"I don't believe *any* man would want to take you apart, my darling. You make an old woman jealous."

Jani laughed. "GiGi," she chastised when her grandmother released her face and went to the refrigerator, "you've always said you were perfectly content with the way you are—that you'd rather be happy than hungry or all dolled up. Now you've changed your mind? Maybe because of your new old boyfriend?"

During the first of these projects to make amends, Jani's brother Cade had put GiGi back into contact with

GiGi's first love, Jonah Morrison. GiGi and Jonah had been high school sweethearts in Northbridge, Montana, where they'd both been raised. The young couple had split up after graduation, and GiGi had subsequently met and married Hank Camden.

But now that both GiGi and Jonah were widowed and coincidentally living in Colorado, they'd reconnected, and they were seeing each other again. Dating—although GiGi complained that she was too old to call it that.

GiGi laughed as she refilled her water glass. "My *new old* boyfriend," she repeated. "Is that what you're all calling Jonah?"

"That's what he is, isn't he?"

"I don't think a man Jonah's age can be called a 'boyfriend.'"

"Your new old suitor? Is that better?"

"You just tend to the man you're supposed to be tending to and don't worry about what to call Jonah," GiGi advised.

"You might be *tending* to Jonah, but I'm not *tending* to any man anymore, let alone the angry Gideon Thatcher," Jani corrected. "I'm just doing what you want me to do—trying to get close enough, often enough, to find some things out about him and his family. I'm not doing anything that might qualify as *tending* to him," she insisted.

"Does he look as good in person as he did in that newspaper picture?" GiGi asked as she slid back into the nook with her refilled glass. "That hardhat he was wearing made it impossible to tell some things—like without it, is he bald and lumpy-headed?"

"No… He has hair," Jani said, instantly picturing

Gideon Thatcher in her mind's eye. It was something that had been happening incessantly since she'd left him on the street the evening before, dragging her into alarmingly involuntary daydreams…

"He has very nice hair," she went on. "Actually, that picture of him in the paper didn't do him justice. And neither did the ones of him on his website. He has great hair—kind of a sandy-brown—"

"Is it neat and clean or does he look like he needs a haircut the way Reggie always did?"

"It's neat and clean. But not so neat that he looks stuffy or severe."

"Clean-shaven or scruffy?"

"Clean-shaven." Leaving that sharply chiseled jawline and that sexy off-center dent in his chin clearly visible. Visible, and such a perfect match to the rest of his bone structure. His face was just rugged enough that he couldn't be considered a pretty-boy—which is what GiGi had called Reggie.

"Is he a big man? He looked like a big man in that picture. Bigger than whoever that was he was shaking hands with," GiGi commented.

"He is a big man. Tall. With broad shoulders." *Impressively* broad shoulders…

"Stocky or lean?"

"Lean. He's not fat in any way."

"Scrawny like Reggie?"

"No, definitely not scrawny, either. I think he was all muscle under the overcoat he was wearing." All muscle and masculinity…

"What about his eyes? What color are his eyes?"

"The most beautiful green you've ever seen—a shimmering sort of sea-green…"

And then it struck Jani that these questions were out of the ordinary and she realized that her grandmother had set a trap for her. A trap she'd fallen into by rhapsodizing somewhat about Gideon Thatcher's appearance. And now GiGi was smiling knowingly.

"Not that I care how he looks," Jani added in an attempt to do damage control. "He could be a troll and it wouldn't matter. He's just the person I need to deal with to do what we need to do. Male, female, good-looking, not good-looking, it doesn't make any difference."

But her grandmother was staring at her from beneath raised eyebrows and still smiling.

In spite of what Jani read in the elderly woman's expression, GiGi said, "No, of course it doesn't make any difference that he looks even better in person than in his pictures. I was just curious."

"*He hates us,* GiGi," Jani repeated, emphasizing each word for effect to warn the older woman away from whatever she was thinking.

"And that's what we're going to try to make up for," GiGi concluded.

"His secretary called this morning to arrange for me to meet him for coffee after work tonight. What am I supposed to do if he just gives me a flat no on our proposal and won't have anything to do with me?"

"He wouldn't need a whole cup of coffee to do that, he could have said that on the phone. Or had his secretary tell you. If he wants to have coffee, I think there's hope."

But what exactly was her grandmother hoping for? Jani wondered.

"I suppose," she agreed. "Although he could just

want a check from us and to never set eyes on me again—what then?"

GiGi laughed. "Persuade him otherwise," she suggested.

Jani rolled her eyes. "Easy for you to say," she muttered.

But that was all she said on the subject. She had to get back to work and, since they were finished eating, she stood to clear the table.

As she did she was thinking about that meeting with Gideon Thatcher tonight, and calculating if she could run by her house to change her clothes before going back to the office.

Because when she'd gotten dressed this morning she hadn't known she would end the day seeing him again.

Now that she knew she would be, she was wishing she'd worn her better butt-hugging slacks.

And the new blouse with the collar that stood high around the column of her neck but didn't quite meet in front until the first button just barely above her cleavage.

It wasn't a work outfit—in fact she never wore anything to work that even hinted at cleavage.

But when it came to Gideon Thatcher she thought she could use all the help she could get.

Just for the cause.

Anything to aid the cause.

Not because she cared how she looked for him...

Chapter Three

Gideon Thatcher was late and Jani's feet hurt.

Not only had she gone home and changed her clothes after having lunch with her grandmother, she'd also changed her shoes. Three-inch heels with toes as pointy as arrows. Like the deep purple blouse with the slit of a plunging neckline, they weren't work shoes. But they looked fabulous so she'd opted to suffer. And luckily the coffee shop Gideon Thatcher had chosen had its own parking lot, so there was no real hike from her car.

Only he wasn't there yet when she arrived—on time at six o'clock—so she was waiting for him at the entrance.

On her feet.

For the past twenty-five minutes.

She was beginning to think he wasn't coming and wondering what she was going to do if he didn't when a jazzy little sports car pulled into the lot, parked next to her car on the passenger side, and out of it stepped the man himself.

Was keeping her waiting a power play? Just another indication that he was going to be difficult?

It didn't matter. She could handle that. It was part of what she did for work.

Handling the way he looked was something else, though. She couldn't keep her eyes from being riveted to him as he headed for the coffee shop.

He was wearing a dark gray suit that was clearly tailor-made for him, accentuating his broad shoulders, his narrow waist and hips, his long, powerful legs.

There was no shadow of beard to mar his sexy, sculpted face. His charcoal-colored tie was still knotted tight against his dove-gray shirt collar. And if a power play was what he had in mind, he was definitely dressed for it because as he came into the coffee shop it was power that he exuded.

But he surprised her by greeting her with an apology that bore not even a hint of arrogance or satisfaction.

"I'm sorry I'm late. I had a meeting with a Lakeview city councilwoman and she was in no hurry to leave."

Maybe the councilwoman was just enjoying the view....

Because Jani still was. In spite of herself.

"No problem," she said, appreciating that his tardiness hadn't been on purpose. But she also noted that his overall attitude continued to be cool and aloof. And not at all friendly.

"Coffees are on the latecomer," he announced with no particular warmth, moving to the counter to order. "Or whatever you want…"

Jani ordered a decaf latte. While Gideon ordered a

plain black coffee for himself, she took off her knee-length wool coat and draped it over her arm.

She looked up to find him watching her much the way she'd been watching him as he'd approached the coffee shop from his car.

He averted his eyes the minute she caught him at it and fidgeted just the slightest bit.

Jani did a quick check of her blouse buttons but they were all fastened; as far as she could tell, nothing was amiss, so she wasn't sure what about the way she looked made him even slightly ill at ease.

She just hoped she didn't look as if she were trying too hard. Or worse yet, as though she were trying to seduce him with the blouse and the shoes. And her better butt-hugging slacks...

Maybe she should put her coat back on. But she was afraid that would seem odd, so she decided she just had to weather whatever was going on with him.

When their coffees were ready they took them to a bistro table in a corner where they sat across from each other. Jani laid her coat over the third, unused chair.

"I was glad you called," she began, opting for friendliness even if he wasn't. "But I would have met you during business hours—I don't want to keep you away from your wife and family..."

Yes, she was fishing. There wasn't a wedding ring but that didn't necessarily mean he wasn't married. Or didn't have kids. And wasn't that the underlying reason she was doing any of this—to get to know the man? It wasn't that she was curious herself....

"I'm divorced," he said curtly, giving her no more information than that. "But I suppose you didn't like leaving your husband home alone."

Was he fishing, too? After all, the lack of a ring on a woman's finger was a dead giveaway, wasn't it? Or had he just not noticed?

She held up her left hand, showing him the back of it. "I'm not married," she said.

But then she recalled spilling the contents of her purse the evening before.

Of course he would assume that a book about getting pregnant would mean there was a husband in the picture.

"Oh, because of the book," she said when light dawned on her. "No, no husband. Not even a fiancé or a boyfriend currently. I'm just not letting that stop me from having a baby."

No, no, no, she hadn't really said that, had she? Unfiltered thoughts right out of her mouth—always a mistake!

Not that she was hiding her plan to have a baby on her own. She'd vowed that if she were going to do it, it would be without making excuses or being ashamed of it. She was going to do it proudly and joyously. The way having a baby should be.

But she was talking to Gideon Thatcher. He was a stranger and a man who didn't like the Camdens on principle. This was not a situation where it was appropriate to talk about her baby plan.

Not that Gideon Thatcher said anything to encourage her to share more information. He was staring into his coffee cup without making any comment at all.

Then he changed the subject. "I've thought about the Camdens wanting to do something for Lakeview in my great-grandfather's name."

All business. *Good,* Jani thought, tasting her own

latte and merely raising her eyebrows at him in question rather than trusting herself to say something else she shouldn't.

"I've been thinking for a while about a community center there," he continued. "Something that offers recreation, low-cost day care and preschool, and adult education to help retrain people who might want to escape working in the Camden factories and warehouses, or develop more skills to help them move up the ladder within your organization. But it isn't in the budget, and I haven't been able to come up with the extra funding."

"The Franklin Thatcher Community Center," Jani suggested.

"I have a building in mind that would meet the requirements, but it's been out of use for over a dozen years and needs some serious repair, remodeling and even some reconstruction. Not to mention landscaping to create sports fields and a playground to serve the day care and preschool. Plus there's staffing, operating costs—"

"But it sounds like something that would really benefit Lakeview and be nice to have your great-grandfather's name on," Jani observed.

"It isn't just a simple park," he pointed out with a challenging arch to one of his own eyebrows.

"No, but it seems worthwhile. Something good to give back to the community." And something that was definitely going to cost...

He relaxed slightly more in his chair and seemed to reach unconsciously for his tie, loosening it, unbuttoning the collar button that had come out from hiding behind it.

Then he stretched his neck a little. His head swayed

to the right, then to the left, his chin jutted forward, and for some reason Jani saw it all in slow motion.

She savored every nuance, finding every detail somehow enticing. And suddenly she felt fidgety herself.

Was that why he'd been fidgeting when she'd taken off her coat? Was it possible that he'd *liked* what he'd seen? That he'd felt enticed by it?

Probably not, she told herself, knowing that she shouldn't entertain such thoughts. Not with this man and not at this juncture in her life.

And yet if the way he looked and the simplest of gestures could entice her, it helped to think that she might be able to entice him a little, too. Anything that gave an inkling that he didn't have complete contempt for her was a plus. It helped her feel as if they were on more equal territory. And she'd take whatever crumbs she could get.

"So, if it's *worthwhile,* are the Camdens willing to foot the bill?" he asked, repeating her term with a tinge of insolence. "Including staff salaries and operating expenses until the center becomes self-supporting?" There was a challenge in his tone, as well.

Jani pretended to consider what he was asking even though her instructions were to do whatever he wanted. He *was* asking a lot, after all. She looked into her own coffee cup. Letting silence reign for a moment, she took another drink of her latte.

Then she said, "Of course I'll have to run the actual numbers by my family, but I think a community center is a great idea and I think they all will, too."

"In my great-grandfather's name? Without strings attached, the Camdens won't profit from it now or at any time in the future—in fact it could be instrumental in costing them warehouse and factory workers. And the donation will be absolutely anonymous, there won't be a single drop of credit to your family.…"

His terms and more challenge.

"Agreed," Jani said simply.

"It's going to cost a hell of a lot more than a park," he warned unnecessarily.

"The money isn't the point," Jani said sincerely. "We just want to do something for the community that honors your great-grandfather."

Gideon Thatcher took a turn at letting silence reign, studying her.

Then he said, "That's some kind of big guilt you people are showing."

Jani met him eye to eye. "I know you believe the worst, but there is another side to this that I might tell you when you're ready to hear it."

"Is that so?"

"It is," she said, holding her ground calmly, quietly, but with conviction.

His great green eyes stayed steady on her for a long moment. While Jani knew he was once again gauging her motives and whether there was some hidden trap or conspiracy in this, she also had the sense that he was looking beyond the fact that she was a Camden and sizing her up as her own person.

His expression didn't reveal the conclusion he came to, though.

"I suppose we should start with you taking a look at the building and getting an idea of what you're signing on for."

Was she imagining it or was there a microscopically small reduction in the hostility in his tone?

She was probably just imagining it because she wanted it to be the case.

"Just tell me where and when," she said.

"So eager…" he muttered, still watching her and again seeming suspicious.

"Actually, I'm just trying to be cooperative," she corrected.

He didn't remark on that. He merely went on watching her as if to say that he'd be the judge. But Jani thought that actions spoke louder than words, and he wouldn't be able to find fault with her actions because she was on the up-and-up.

Then, out of the blue, he said, "So you're not married.…"

"Nope, never have been."

"But you're not letting the lack of a husband—or even a fiancé or a boyfriend—stop you from having a family?"

"Not anymore."

"That's a bold move."

Oh yeah, he was sizing her up.

She shrugged. "Sometimes it feels that way," she admitted. "But I just started the process. I've only had my first visit to the doctor, and I'm taking it one step at a time." Which was what she told herself whenever the prospect of artificial insemination, pregnancy, delivery and raising a child alone seemed daunting.

One step at a time. Take it one step at a time and you can handle it.…

It was actually the advice GiGi had given all ten of her grandchildren whenever they'd thought anything was insurmountable, and it had always served Jani well.

"I suppose you *are* a Camden—you don't need financial help," Gideon said. "But still… Will there even be a father in the picture?" He suddenly sat up straighter and leaned farther back in his chair, held up his hands, palms out, and added, "None of my business. I'm out of line."

"No, it's okay," Jani said, thinking that if she needed him to eventually open up to her, it might aid the cause for her to be open with him first. "There *won't* be a father in the picture. There will only be me. And a baby!" she said enthusiastically.

He was looking even more intently at her, with the shadow of a frown putting a small crease between his eyebrows. "Do you think that a father in a kid's life is just inconsequential?" he asked as if it were an issue to him.

"No! Not at all," Jani said. "I loved my own dad dearly—I was an awful daddy's girl. And regardless of how you think of H.J., I loved him, too—he was an important man in my life. So was a man named Louie, who was sort of a substitute father when I needed him to be. This is just…" She wanted to foster a sense of openness with Gideon but she wasn't willing to be *too* open or go into too many details, either.

"…this is just what I've decided to do. A baby is something I've wanted forever and I'm not going to wait any longer to have one. Kids grow up in all sorts of different situations now—lots and lots of them in one-parent homes. If…" no, she wasn't going to have defeatist thoughts "…*when* I get pregnant, I'll just love my baby enough for it to *feel* like it has two parents."

The crease between Gideon's eyes deepened. It reminded Jani of the way Gigi responded to this subject.

"I know not everyone approves—my grandmother

wishes I wouldn't do it," she said. "But things don't always work out the way we—or anyone else—wish they would."

"True…"

"So sometimes you just have to do what you have to do to get what you want."

"H. J. Camden's philosophy?" Gideon said with challenge in his tone again.

I walked into that one, didn't I?

"Family *was* important to my great-grandfather," she said, purposely misinterpreting Gideon's words and ignoring what he'd actually meant. "And having a family is really, really important to me, too. *That's* why I'm not going to wait or leave it to chance anymore."

"I can't say that leaving things to chance has worked out for me," he said. Then he shrugged. "Well, good luck with that, I guess."

"Thank you," she answered as if his wishes had been more heartfelt.

He asked if she wanted a second latte but when Jani declined he said, "I should probably get going. I have paperwork to do yet tonight."

Why did it sound as if he might be reluctant to end this? Jani wondered. It certainly didn't *seem* as if he were having a good time with her.

Maybe he just wanted to put off working more tonight.

He stood up and took their empty cups to throw in the trash, leaving Jani with confirmation that he did, indeed, have manners.

And an incredibly good rear end that came into view when he bent over to pick up a package of napkins one of the teenage employees dropped when he walked by carrying more of them than he could balance.

But admiring Gideon Thatcher's derriere was totally uncalled for and when Jani realized that was what she was doing, she stood, too, and began to put on her coat.

Her gaze remained on Gideon, though, even after he was standing straight and tall again. As she admired the drape of his suit coat from those expansive shoulders to his narrow waist and hips, she somehow kept missing the opening of her second coat sleeve.

She was still fumbling with it as he got back to the table and he gave her an assist, holding her coat up to make the armhole more accessible.

"Thanks," she said for the second time, ultra-aware of his arm stretched across her back.

It wasn't as if he were putting his arm *around* her, she told herself.

It just sort of felt that way.

And sent a little tingle through her that she had no control over. That was silly. And uncalled for.

And still somehow made her feel all warm inside...

Which was just plain crazy.

Then he took his arm away and it was even crazier that she was sorry it was gone.

"So, looking at the building for the community center," she said to put things squarely back into the dominion of business.

"Right..." Gideon said, giving no indication that being near her had affected him the way it had affected her. "I'll be in Lakeview all day tomorrow. I could meet you at the building I have in mind at...maybe, let's say, four-thirty? Any earlier and I'm afraid I might keep you waiting again."

"My schedule is light tomorrow. I can leave work early enough to get to Lakeview by four-thirty. Just send me the address."

"I'll do that," he agreed as they headed for the coffee shop exit.

"Thanks for the latte," Jani said, passing in front of him as he held the door open for her. "And I'm glad you decided to let us do this for Lakeview and for your great-grandfather."

The frown that skittered across his handsome face made her wonder if, for just a few minutes, he'd forgotten who she was. And she was sorry she'd brought it back to mind.

His only acknowledgment of what she'd said was to raise that dented chin of his as he followed her outside.

She had the sense that he was tempted to walk her to the driver's side of her car when he hesitated to go to his own. But apparently he resisted the urge because as Jani went to her sedan, he walked in front of it to his own vehicle.

While Jani unlocked her door he stood with his back to his, watching her.

"I'll see you tomorrow," she called across to him.

"Right. Tomorrow," he confirmed, waiting for her to get in before he turned to his own car.

Sitting in her driver's seat, Jani got her second glimpse of his rear end through her passenger window as he leaned over to unlock his door.

But she quickly turned her head to face forward when he got in so he wouldn't catch her ogling him.

As she started her engine and pulled out of the parking spot, she angled her eyes in the direction of her rearview mirror so he wouldn't know she was looking—even though she was. She just couldn't stop herself from getting every last glimpse of him.

The thought of seeing him again the next day excited her a little.

Maybe even more than a little.

In fact, she was already looking forward to it as if it were the highlight of the day to come.

And wondering if she should wear the formfitting fuchsia dress that she usually considered too tight and way, way too short for the office…

Chapter Four

The site Gideon had in mind for the community center was Lakeview's old city and county building. It was a plain, three-story yellow-brick structure with boards over several windows, grounds that were all weeds and a cracked and pitted parking lot.

Jani didn't have any trouble finding it on Wednesday afternoon—it was on the same road that led to the Camden warehouses and factories. She must have driven past it on the few occasions she'd been to the facilities in Lakeview. She just hadn't taken any notice.

As she drove up, what initially struck her was that Gideon hadn't been kidding about it needing a lot of work. But then she spotted the parking lot, Gideon's sports car and Gideon himself, and everything else flew out of her mind.

Wearing tan slacks and a short leather jacket over a cocoa-colored shirt, he was half sitting, half leaning on the hood of his car. His long legs were stretched far out in front of him and crossed at the ankles. His arms were locked over his chest, his hair was slightly windblown. And had the backdrop been more scenic, it could have been an ad in *GQ* for the car or the clothes. Or the man himself. He looked dashing with just a hint of bad boy thrown in to make it interesting.

That's the picture that should be on his website, Jani thought as she parked alongside of him and tried to get her pulse to stop racing. She reminded herself that this was not a social visit, that Gideon Thatcher reviled her and her family and that she had way too much on her own personal agenda to be distracted by him. Gideon Thatcher was just one little compartment that she had to deal with in the whole spectrum of things.

But that first glimpse of him made it difficult to recall that anything else existed. In her life, on her agenda or in any other way.

Especially when her heart was beating at such an accelerated pace.

She took a deep breath as she turned off the ignition and ordered herself to just calm down.

"Am I late?" she asked when she got out of her car, quickly slipping on the hip-length jacket she hadn't wanted to wear while she was driving.

Gideon shoved off his hood. "No, I wanted to get here ahead of you to turn on some power, maybe get a little heat going in there so it wouldn't be too miserable to walk around." His eyes dropped to where her legs were generously displayed below the short hem of her fuchsia dress. "Looks like it's a good thing I did or you might have frozen to death."

It sounded as if he were trying to be critical but

somehow missed the boat. Maybe because his gaze lingered on her legs and Jani recognized appreciation when she saw it.

Then he raised his green eyes to her face and said, "Be warned, it isn't a pretty sight inside. Looks like kids have broken in and partied, and there's been some wildlife activity, too—mice, a raccoon, maybe, and I found a dead squirrel on the third floor. I threw an old newspaper over it, but in case you're inclined to touch anything, my advice is not to."

Jani held up her hands, palms out, then made a show of putting them in the pockets of her jacket. "Noted," she announced.

He nodded in the direction of her three-inch heels. "And watch your step in those things—there are cracks in the cement all around here."

Again the words were purely precautionary but a split-second lingering of his gaze told her that he wasn't otherwise opposed to the black suede shoes that accentuated her ankles and calves.

"Oh, don't worry, I'm so used to heels I could climb Mount Kilimanjaro in them," she assured him.

Just then her heel caught in a crumbling spot in the parking lot, and she would have gone down had Gideon not grabbed her arm in the steadying grip of one big hand.

"Okay, maybe not," she said with an embarrassed laugh, hating that she seemed to be such a klutz around this man.

"Are you okay?" he asked.

"Fine," she said, trying to ignore how much she liked having his hand on her arm. And how much she didn't like it when he took it away. "I'll just be more careful."

Maybe by watching where she was going instead of looking at him…

He must not have trusted her, though, because he stayed close, walking beside and slightly behind her as they went up to the old building, as if he were there to catch her should she lose her footing again.

He really does think I'm clumsy….

It wasn't an image she wanted to project so she was extra cautious climbing the steps to the building.

When they reached the wide double doors, Gideon opened one of them and waited for her to go in before following. It was warmer inside than out but not by much, and there was only the dim glow of light shining through aged and dusty globes. But one quick glance around made Jani think that was a blessing—she didn't really want to be able to see too many details.

Gideon launched into tour-guide mode, pointing out the good and the bad, outlining what he had in mind for room after room, floor after floor of the musty-smelling building.

It was actually a little creepy to be there and it occurred to Jani that had she not been with Gideon, she might have been more unnerved by the dusty, cobweb-laced, littered and decaying old place. But there was something about his presence that made her feel less uneasy.

Having once been Lakeview's only courtroom, the third floor was one large open space. When they arrived there, Gideon warned her around the sheet of newspaper hiding the dead squirrel and led her to the windows that weren't broken and boarded up. The glass in them was dirty and sometimes cracked, but from that height they could look down on the surrounding area.

After talking about the need to completely dig up the parking lot and repave it, Gideon pointed out the best positioning for the sports fields and the play park on the grounds below.

Jani asked a few questions but mainly let Gideon talk, basking in the sound of his deep, deep voice, in the fact that when he was talking about his work, his plans, all animosity, all suspicion of her, seemed to fall away. And liking that too much, too.

When the tour was complete, he summed things up for her as they descended the multiple flights of stairs to get back to where they'd begun. It was a daunting list that lost Jani somewhere between new wiring and bringing everything up to current codes.

"Are you sure it wouldn't be easier—and cheaper— to just build a new facility?" she asked as they stepped off the last stair and a piece of marble dropped to the floor behind them.

"Then you'd have demolition expenses and construction costs that you won't have here," Gideon explained. "Besides, the building itself has history for Lakeview— shouldn't a gift *to* the community carry some meaning *for* the community?"

"The city and county building…" Jani mused rather than answering his question because she had the feeling that there was some hidden meaning in this for Gideon, too. "Was this where your great-grandfather's office was when he was mayor?"

"As a matter of fact it was," Gideon confirmed. "It was something he was proud of—he was king of the hill here."

"Then you're right, this is the building that should carry his name," she agreed.

"Speaking of which…" Gideon said, as if she'd provided him with an opening he'd been waiting for her to provide. "I'm going to need to clear that name before Lakeview will want it on anything."

That was a glitch that Jani hadn't expected.

But before she could think of what to say, Gideon told her to wait there while he went down to the boiler room to switch off the breakers and shut the building down again.

He turned and left.

And just when Jani should have been thinking about this new complication, she instead found herself watching him go—specifically, gawking at his rear end. His suit coat had camouflaged it somewhat the night before, but today, with his jacket barely brushing his waist, she had a clear view of his backside. And oh, but it was a fabulous derriere accentuated perfectly in a pair of well-made pants!

This whole project would have been much simpler if the guy just wasn't so distractingly handsome and well built, she thought once he was out of sight and she got hold of herself again.

Then the building went dark, and although Jani hadn't realized there was any sound, it also went silent, leaving the echo of Gideon's steps to announce his return even before he rejoined her at the door.

He held one of the double panels open for her, and Jani stepped out into the pink blush of dusk beginning to fall.

She hadn't noticed until then that she'd been breathing shallowly to avoid the various smells of the old building and whatever was decaying inside of it, but once outside, she took a deep breath. And discovered that the air was rich with the aroma of fresh donuts.

"It definitely smells better out here!" she said.

"Donut shop across the street," Gideon responded, aiming a long index finger in the direction of a strip mall. "Most of your employees at the factories and the warehouses pass by here on their way to and from work—I was in the donut shop yesterday and the owner is talkative. He told me that he bakes fresh for the morning arrivals and again for quitting time, and made sure that he had a drive-through so commuters can get their donut fix without even leaving their cars. See the line already backing up along the side…" He pointed at the busy drive-through window. "And his donuts are great," he added as he slipped his hand into the pocket of his jacket.

"Since you bought last night, how about I treat to donuts now and you can tell me more about clearing your great-grandfather's name," Jani suggested, not eager to get into the subject, but knowing she was going to have to and wanting to get it over with. And thinking that donuts could only help.

"Okay," Gideon said without skipping a beat. "Walk or drive?"

"It's just across the street. I think—if I really work at it—that I can make it without falling on my face if we walk," she said, joking about her own previous displays of gracelessness.

And Gideon Thatcher cracked the slightest of smiles.

Which thrilled Jani more than she could understand. And—unreasonable as it might have been—made spilling her purse, and fumbling to get her coat on at the coffee shop the night before, and nearly falling in the parking lot earlier, all worth it.

"Let's give it a shot then," he said as if he doubted her abilities and they set off across the cracked and crumbling cement walkway that led from the building's entrance to the road.

They made it to the donut shop without incident. The owner greeted Gideon as if he were an old friend and announced that today's donuts and coffee were on the house.

Then he left Jani and Gideon alone to take their coffee and donuts to a corner booth where they both removed their coats.

As Jani slipped into her side of the booth she could see that Gideon was having a good long look at the fuchsia dress that hugged her every curve like a wetsuit. Unless she was mistaken, he seemed to have some trouble taking his eyes off of her.

He managed, though, by concentrating on drinking his steaming coffee.

Still, Jani was happy that she'd opted for the dress and the shoes today, and she fought a smile as she tasted the donut.

It was crispy on the outside, light and cakey on the inside, glazed with a hint of orange—one bite and Jani rhapsodized over the luscious delight.

Gideon agreed that his was delectable, too, before he got down to the business at hand.

"Lakeview has a monthly newspaper that's doing an article next month—a past and present piece—on me and my great-grandfather. It's been scheduled since before you showed up with your park idea and I've already met with the reporter a few times. The part on my great-grandfather will make it clear that what he promised Lakeview all those years ago, he promised in good faith, that he was *not* in H. J. Camden's pocket."

"Will the article be smearing *my* great-grandfather's name in the process?" Jani asked, wondering if he was giving her a heads-up.

"That isn't the slant, no. The paper doesn't want to be sued by the Camdens, that's for sure. And while no one is happy that Lakeview's economy ended up depending on your factories and warehouses, that's still how it is, and no one wants to bite the hand that feeds it, either. It'll be the plain-and-simple facts that Franklin Thatcher believed what he said, what he promised his constituents. That he'd met with the developers H. J. Camden was supposedly bringing in, he saw the plans and proposals with his own eyes. That everything he promised in return for allowing those warehouses and factories to be built, he firmly believed would be taken care of, and that it was completely out of his hands when it wasn't."

"Okay..." Jani said with reservation, wondering if Gideon was merely giving her information or if he wanted something from her.

Then she found out.

"But I'm thinking that a quote from you that confirms that what my great-grandfather did, he did in all honesty, would help exonerate him. A from-the-horse's-mouth kind of thing—"

"Except that the *horse*—H.J.—died in 1996, so it would only be coming from the descendant of the horse."

"Still, confirmation lends credence. Especially a quote from a Camden that confirms that to the best of Franklin Thatcher's knowledge, the factories and warehouses were supposed to be followed by the rest of the development H. J. Camden promised."

"I can confirm that because it was true," Jani said without hesitation.

Once again that seemed to raise some suspicion in Gideon's green eyes. "You're admitting that H.J. duped my great-grandfather?"

Jani shook her head. "It was true that your great-grandfather believed that development would follow the warehouses and factories because it *was* H.J.'s plan," Jani said.

"Uh-huh, and sometime when I'm ready to hear it, you're going to tell me about that," Gideon said facetiously, reiterating what she'd said to him before.

"Right." But she could see that he wasn't receptive to hearing it yet.

"This isn't an opportunity for you to win H. J. Camden points," he warned. "The writer is a friend of mine, so if you try to slip in a single word to make H.J. look good or to make my great-grandfather take any of the fall—"

"I won't. I'll be in complete agreement that Franklin Thatcher was on the up-and-up."

Gideon studied her the way he had on every other occasion they'd met, as if trying to read between the lines because he didn't trust her.

But Jani just weathered his scrutiny, as usual.

At least it didn't seem to take him as long as it had previously to accept that she meant what she said. She counted that as making some progress with him.

"Once my great-grandfather's name is cleared and he goes back to being seen as what he genuinely was— someone who loved Lakeview, who wanted the best for it, and thought what he was doing was going to accomplish that—then a building with his name on it, honoring him, makes more sense. As it is now, why would Lakeview want something honoring the mayor they essentially ran out of town?"

Lakeview had run Franklin Thatcher out of town?

Oh, dear...

"You're right," Jani said without hesitation, realizing only then that it hadn't occurred to either her or to GiGi that there might be the need to restore Franklin Thatcher's name in advance of honoring him.

"I'm sorry," Jani added then, deciding to use this as an opening. "We only know H.J.'s side of things, we don't know what happened to your great-grandfather in the aftermath of the broken promises. Or to the rest of your family, either."

She saw Gideon's jaw clench but he didn't say anything to enlighten her. Obviously it was going to take more to draw that information out of him. This was something that made him angry. But he seemed to be containing that anger for the first time, so maybe she was making some headway with him.

Giving up the hope of learning everything at once, she opted for starting with an easier topic and said, "The part of the article that will be about you... What slant will that take?"

"So far my *interviews* have mainly been my friend and me talking about the Thatcher Group, how that came to be," Gideon said, finishing his donut and focusing on his coffee.

"How *did* the Thatcher Group come to be?" Jani asked.

He still seemed to be struggling to suppress his

anger, so he didn't rush to answer that question. For a moment he merely stared at his hand around the paper cup as if he might not give her the courtesy of a response.

But after a moment, Jani had the impression that he'd set that anger aside and when he answered his tone was neutral.

"I got my degree in architecture—"

"Where?"

"University of Colorado in Denver. I had to pay my own way through, so I couldn't afford Boulder campus."

"You worked your way through college *and* grad school? No scholarships or grants or loans?"

"I got a few small scholarships and grants, but I tried to avoid loans. Instead I had a low-paying internship with a downtown architect—an alumni of the Denver campus who had had to pay his own tuition, too. He was—and is—a tough old bird, but he takes on one paid intern to help them out. It's something we do, too. A payback. I couldn't have made it through without that help, so we have a program that offers the same thing to kids in that situation."

"That might be something we'd be interested in contributing to, too," Jani said, glad to see another opening where she might be able to make amends.

But Gideon shook his head. "It's funded through the Thatcher Group. We don't take donations for it."

Jani had the sense that even if he did, he wouldn't accept donations for that from the Camdens. That accepting the community center for Lakeview and to honor his great-grandfather was as far as he was willing to go. So she didn't push it.

Instead she said, "Did you go to work for the 'tough old bird' when you graduated?"

"I did. But my goal was to have my own office, my own firm, so going to work for Mathias was just to learn all I could, get some experience under my belt and save money."

"How long did you work for him?"

"Five years. Long enough to figure out that I didn't want my company to be limited to architecture."

"You didn't like doing what you'd gotten two degrees to do?"

"I did. I loved it. I still do most of our building design work. But I also wanted to do more than that—to serve a broader base of clients and design entire communities. To focus on urban development, not just on a single building here and there—"

"You wanted to do city planning."

"Exactly. It's like the community center," he said with a nod toward the window that faced the run-down old building. "Sure I could bulldoze and design something else, but I like that that building has some history to it, a meaning in the landscape where it's stood for generations. I want to see the whole picture, past, present and future. I want to do more than erect just one nice building. I want to create whole communities that serve all the needs of the people who live in them while still leaving them memories of what came before and inspiration for what they can do from there—"

He screwed up his handsome face into a self-deprecating sort of grimace. "I didn't mean to wax philosophic and sound so—"

"Like you really do love what you do?" Jani supplied

before he could put himself down. She admired his passion for what he did.

"I do love it," he concluded as if to avoid showing too much more of himself to her.

"And you're successful at it—I saw on your website that you've worked all over the world."

"We do okay," he said with humility. "It's put me in the position to rectify what happened in Lakeview, and that's important to me."

Jani had the feeling as he spoke that he was reminding himself of who she was and why they were there, of the past he didn't want to let go of.

She didn't try to distract him. "Actually, after reading your credits and awards on the website and a few other articles I found about the Thatcher Group's work, I was surprised that you'd take on a project as small as Lakeview. It's really kind of a coup for them to get you. You've done a lot of things that were bigger and a whole lot more high-profile."

"All that helped me get this project when just the name Thatcher was enough for Lakeview's sitting city council to say no. I had to do a lot of lobbying for this and if the Thatcher Group *didn't* have the reputation and standing it has, I probably wouldn't have been hired anyway. As it was, I still had to underbid the lowest bidder and make promises to organize some extra fundraising to sell them on me."

"Not something you have to do to get all your jobs, I'm sure."

"I don't have to do that to get *any* other jobs. But when the Lakeview redevelopment project came on the radar I knew it was my chance to do what my great-grandfather wanted done for Lakeview in the first place.

It was also the opportunity to redeem the Thatcher name."

"Was that important to anyone in your family before you?" Jani asked cautiously, curious but unsure if the question would offend him.

"It was important to *everyone* before me. But I'm the first to be able to do anything about it."

"That isn't *why* you went into architecture in the first place, is it? With far-off hopes of fixing things in Lakeview? Would you have rather been a ballet dancer or something?"

The faint smile again. It really wasn't much of anything and yet spotting it was still enough to send little shards of delight through Jani.

"A ballet dancer?" Gideon asked. "Of all the occupations, you're wondering if I might have wanted to be that?"

"Well," Jani said, smiling slightly herself for the first time, "even if you had become a doctor or a dentist or a lawyer or something, you still could have set up shop in Lakeview and helped the people and their economy that way. But there wouldn't have been any way to use ballet dancing to help Lakeview. Unless they have a ballet troupe and I don't know it."

"They don't. And no, I didn't become an architect just to get to do what my great-grandfather wanted done in Lakeview. It was what I was interested in and it just happened to put me in a position to help. Which I'm grateful for now."

"I do think they're lucky to have you," Jani said quietly, meaning it but worrying that he might think she was just blowing smoke to flatter him.

She didn't see the usual signs that he was put off

but he did seem slightly uncomfortable with the compliment. Uncomfortable enough to change the subject.

"What about you? College or just the family business?" he asked, surprising her by showing interest rather than animosity toward her.

"I went to the University of Southern California in Los Angeles. It had the highest-rated program for public relations. And it was California—sunshine and beaches and celebrities—it sounded like the most fun."

"Was it?"

He'd worked his way through college and struggled while she'd had it easy. Jani felt guilty for admitting it, but she didn't want to lie to him, so she said, "It was fun. But my older brother Cade nearly flunked out of his first year of college because of too much partying and I'd already seen that my grandmother wouldn't put up with it, so I studied hard and basically kept my nose clean."

"And graduated with a bachelor's degree or more?"

"I have a bachelor's degree in public relations, a master's degree in marketing."

"All aimed at working in the family business," he assumed.

"Yeah," she admitted. "H.J. helped my grandmother raise us—me, my three brothers and my six cousins— and he did a lot of talking about our responsibility to take over the family business. We all grew up knowing that working for Camden Incorporated was what we were supposed to do. GiGi—"

"GiGi?"

"Oh, sure, you wouldn't know who that is. 'GiGi' is what we call our grandmother. Her name is Georgianna and somewhere along the way one of the older grandkids shortened *Grandma Georgianna* to GiGi.

Anyway, GiGi reinforced H.J.'s lectures about taking over the company by making sure we all knew that a lot of people depended on the Camdens to make their living and so, yes, we did have a responsibility to keep things going."

"Did *you* want to be a ballet dancer instead?" he asked with just that hint of a smile and Jani suddenly found herself wanting badly to see the full version.

A full smile was what she finally gave him.

"You've seen how graceful I am," she joked at her own expense.

That brought a slightly wider curve to his supple lips but still not the unreserved grin she was hoping for. It was something, though—one more small step—and Jani was glad to see it.

"So not a ballet dancer," he said. "But was there another occupation you would have chosen if you weren't a Camden who had to go to work for the family business?"

"Actually, we were all raised knowing we were expected to work for the family business, but choosing what we do for it was completely up to each of us individually. If I had wanted to be an architect, for instance, I could have been. Then I would have designed Camden Superstores and facilities and office buildings. What each of us wanted to do, we've done, we've just done it for the family business. I liked public relations and marketing, so I head public relations and marketing."

"And who runs the family business as a whole?"

"There are ten grandchildren—we make up the board of directors and we all have one vote on everything. My brother Cade holds the title of CEO, but in fact he doesn't have any more power than any of us. H.J. set it up that way and so far it's worked. I guess it helps that we're a very close family. We get along, we were taught to cooperate with each other and we all just basically like each other."

"I'm an only child so I guess I don't have much of a concept of that," Gideon said.

As they'd been sitting there, the donut shop had filled up considerably and there were now people searching for free tables. And there Jani and Gideon were, taking up a booth when they'd finished their coffee and donuts.

So, as reluctant as she was to end what had turned into a normal, pleasant conversation with Gideon, Jani said, "We should probably eat more donuts or get going…"

She was half hoping that Gideon might actually want another donut and would give her the excuse to draw this out a little longer. But when he looked around and seemed to notice for the first time that they weren't alone in the place, he began to gather their empty coffee cups, napkins and the tissue paper the donuts had been served on.

"Yeah, I guess we have been taking up space for longer than we should have."

As Gideon disposed of everything, Jani stood and put her coat on so she was ready to go when he returned to the booth and grabbed his own jacket, slipping it on as they left the shop.

"If you're still on board with the community center," he said as they went across the street again, "I can have preliminary paperwork drawn up by Friday—a proposal of what needs to be done, an estimate of what it will cost. We can go over it and then you can take it back to your family. If they still want to put up the money, I'll get things started."

"We will," Jani assured him as they reached their cars. He escorted her to the driver's side of hers this time.

She unlocked her door and opened it but didn't get in as she said, "When do you want to go over the paperwork? I'm swamped all day Friday, but we could do it over dinner Friday night, if you're free. I'll put it on my expense account and we'll make it a dinner meeting.…"

There wasn't a single part of that that Jani had thought about before she'd said it. Including that Friday night was not a time for a business dinner. Her mouth had just run away with her while her brain had been busy thinking about when she was going to see him again. And wanting it to be sooner rather than later.

Then she realized she'd just basically asked him out, and even if it had been under the pretext of going over the paperwork, that wasn't actually what was prompting her to do it.

"I'm free for dinner Friday night," Gideon said with surprisingly little hesitation.

Well. Okay then…

"There's a great place, a Tuscan grill, near the Cherry Creek mall—"

He said the name of it before she did and agreed that it was a good meeting place. "What time?" he asked.

"Seven-thirty?" She was more inclined toward dinner at eight, which would make it easier to run home after work and change clothes. But somehow an eight-o'clock dinner seemed more datelike, while a seven-thirty dinner had a bit more of a business feel, and the fact that it was already taking place on a Friday seemed to call for at least that much reserve.

"Seven-thirty is fine. I'll meet you there."

"Great."

And why it suddenly seemed like they'd just been on a date, Jani didn't know. But standing in the parking lot in the early darkness, looking up at Gideon, the question of kissing flashed through her mind as if that's exactly what they'd been doing.

Kissing?

Of course not. It was out of the question.

But still her gaze went to his mouth. To his full lips. And she wondered…

She just couldn't help it.

She wondered what kind of kisser he might be. Good? Bad? Mediocre? Dry? Wet and sloppy? Just right…

She'd never know.

Of course she'd never know.

But somehow, deep, deep down, a little part of her regretted that.

Which was ridiculous, she told herself.

"Okay then…" she said, realizing only in that moment that Gideon had been staring at her, too. Much the way she'd been staring at him…

But probably not with thoughts of kissing.

He doesn't like me.

Although he wasn't looking at her as if he didn't like her…

Still, this was going nowhere because it had nowhere to go, so she said, "Friday night. Seven-thirty."

"Preliminary paperwork in hand," he added, his voice slightly deeper, slightly quieter than she'd ever heard it, as if he were reminding himself of their business together.

Then he said, "See you then," and went around to the driver's side of his sports car, getting in only after he glanced across the top to make sure Jani had gotten into her sedan.

She waved, knowing she had no reason to have continued to watch him, and turned to look out her windshield while she started her engine.

Another glance in his direction found him looking straight ahead while he did the same, and Jani took that as her cue to put her car into gear and leave.

And yet as she drove through rush-hour traffic to get back to Denver, her mind wasn't really on the slow-moving, bumper-to-bumper crawl that got her onto the highway.

It was still on Gideon Thatcher.

And her curiosity about what kind of a kisser he might be…

Chapter Five

"It's a dinner *meeting,* not a dinner date. I'll be paying and putting it on my expense account," Jani insisted to her cousins.

Livi and Lindie had dropped by her house on their way to a movie Friday evening to ask what she'd learned at her doctor's appointment that afternoon.

But they'd come in on Jani getting ready for her seven-thirty dinner with Gideon and accused her of prepping for a date.

"The soup cans say you're lying," Livi said, pointing to the empty metal containers that Jani had her hair wrapped around as it dried from the quick shampoo she'd done in the shower when she'd rushed home.

"Homecoming junior year of high school. Prom that same year. The Sweetheart Dance when we were seniors," Lindie added. "Those are the times you went to the trouble of using soup cans to make the waves of your hair bigger, so they're softer and sleeker and—"

"Sexier—that's what you said," Livi finished her sister's sentence. "Why do you want to be soft and sleek and sexy for a dinner *meeting?*"

"I just wanted a little different look, okay? Without the damage of the heating tools. I remembered the soup cans and thought I'd try them again, that's all. I told you guys the same thing I told GiGi and the boys—Gideon Thatcher is one of those people in the hate-the-Camdens camp. Top it off with the fact that I've taken myself out of the dating pool and put myself on the mommy track, and all you have here is a dinner *meeting.*"

One she was looking forward to, but still nothing *more* than a meeting—that's what Jani had been telling herself since she'd set it up.

"GiGi says he has green eyes," Livi prodded. "Reggie had green eyes. You're a sucker for green eyes...."

"I'm a sucker for babies. Reggie cured me of being a sucker for anything else."

"I have a friend who spotted Reggie on a plane to Las Vegas last weekend," Lindie said as if she'd been debating about whether or not to tell Jani. "Just in case you have any doubts that you did the right thing..."

"Believe me, after four years of frustration and then being scared to death thanks to Reggie, I don't have any doubt that I was right to finally call it off with him. And the last thing I'm interested in is starting all over again with another guy and putting off what I really want. Again. So I'm telling you, tonight is a dinner meeting and that's it!"

"So *is* there going to be a baby?" Livi asked, conceding the point and getting to the subject that made

Jani happier. What her cousins had come tonight to ask about in the first place.

"With any luck, yes, there will be a baby," Jani confirmed. "My tests and blood work were all good, so I have the go-ahead. The next step is to pick a donor, then I'll start the hormones and—"

"We could have a baby by this time next year!" Lindie finished for her.

"Fingers crossed…" Jani said, thankful that her cousins were supportive.

Lindie, Livi and their brother, Lang, were the Camden triplets. The triplets had been born the same year as Jani—they were the youngest of the Camden grandchildren. They'd lived together with GiGi from the time they were six. And while all ten of the cousins were as close as siblings, since Jani, Livi and Lindie were the only girls, they were particularly close. Her female cousins felt like sisters to Jani, and what they thought of her plan to have a baby on her own was important to her. Vital to her, actually.

And they were in favor of it.

"How do you pick a donor?" Lindie asked. "Do you go to a sperm bank or something?"

"The doctor has an affiliation with one he trusts— not only because of the donors they use and their screening process, but also because of the way the sperm is handled. He says *viability* can depend on things like that. So yes, the sperm comes from a sperm bank, but I do it through the doctor. I'll go into the office to read profiles next Wednesday and choose."

"Pick a dad, any dad…" Lindie joked, sounding like a carnival hustler. Then her eyes widened and she said, "Oh, that probably sounded *bad!* I'm sorry!"

Jani didn't take offense. She knew that what she was planning to do was uncharted territory—it was for her, and it certainly was for her family. They were all just feeling their way, so she didn't hold it against anyone if they said something awkward.

Instead she held up two different outfit options to give her cousins something else to talk about. "The blue dress or the sweater and slacks?"

"The blue dress if it's a date. The sweater and slacks if it's just a casual dinner *meeting*," Lindie said.

"So the sweater and slacks," Jani decreed, regretting that she hadn't just put on the blue dress without asking for their opinion.

"GiGi said this guy is giving you a hard time?" Livi commented as Jani pulled on the white cowl-necked angora sweater and the gray pinstripe pants.

"It was a little better when I saw him on Wednesday, but like I said, he's definitely in the hate-the-Camdens camp."

She'd put on blush and mascara already, and now took the soup cans out of her hair. After brushing it, it did fall in softer waves around her shoulders, so the technique had worked the way she remembered it.

"Hey, the soup cans really do work!" Livi marveled.

All of the Camden grandchildren bore a striking resemblance to one another but that was particularly true of the girls—something that had made it difficult for their classmates in elementary school to believe that Lang was the other triplet and not Jani.

"Can I borrow them?" Lindie asked. "I have a blind date tomorrow night and no time to run to the store for soup."

"Sure," Jani said, thinking that if there was a chance

she might be seeing Gideon again soon she might not want to part with them. But she could hardly say *that!*

"We should take off or we'll be late for the movie," Livi said.

"Let me get a bag to carry the soup cans," Jani offered, and they all left her bedroom.

"You look great, by the way," Lindie said as they went to the kitchen. "Wear those new black heels you bought when we were shopping last Saturday… Oh, or is this guy short? You don't want to tower above him, that'll only make him more intimidated."

"He's not short *or* intimidated, believe me," Jani said of Gideon.

"He's not short and has green eyes…" Livi said as if she'd heard something in Jani's tone to provoke a return to the initial suspicion that tonight's dinner was a date. "Is it possible that even though this guy is in the hate-the-Camdens camp, you aren't so much in the hate-the-guy camp?"

"I don't hate him. Why would I hate him?" Jani said, hearing the overcompensation in her own tone.

"Do you *like* him?" Lindie asked, suspicious again, too.

"I don't have any personal opinion about him one way or another. This is just my turn up to bat on one of these missions and I'm trying to get it over and done with so I can just concentrate on the baby. I'm not letting anything keep me from having a baby anymore— tall with green eyes or not," she said firmly.

"And you shouldn't," Livi agreed.

"I can't wait to be able to start buying baby clothes!" Lindie added, obviously trying to compensate for her earlier insensitivity.

"And to decorate the nursery," Livi put in.

"What do we need men for?" Lindie again.

"Yeah, they're nice, but they're like jewelry—accessories, not necessities," Livi said.

Jani put the soup cans in a sack and kept quiet, knowing that neither of her cousins actually believed what they were saying about men and that they were both just trying to put a good face on things for Jani's sake.

It wasn't that she didn't want a man in her life or that she thought they were nothing more than accessories. But she'd done everything she could with Reggie to stick it out, to make it work, so she could arrive at the point of having a baby with him. With a husband.

But that had failed. And this was what she was left needing to do. Or risk never having a baby of her own.

So no, no man.

Sure, she preferred to have a family the old-fashioned way. The traditional way.

And if Gideon Thatcher came to mind at that very moment?

It wasn't as if there was a connection.

Regardless of what her traitorous brain might be throwing out at her, she was done fostering any kind of illusions.

And that's exactly what it would be to so much as entertain the idea that—even if she had the time to wait for something to develop between them—Gideon Thatcher would ever be inclined to father a Camden baby.

"Uh… Are they giving those away in there?"

After eating their meal of luscious lasagna and going over paperwork, Jani had left Gideon to go to the ladies' room. She'd gone in with only her purse, but now she emerged carrying a tiny, sleeping baby boy in her arms.

Just then the baby's mother came out of the ladies' room holding a crying three-year-old, and Jani nodded in her direction. "I'm just helping out," she said to Gideon, waiting for the woman to catch up to her so she could follow her to her table and hand the baby over to the father.

When Jani was done, she sat back down, replaced her napkin in her lap and explained. "While Mom was changing the baby's diaper the three-year-old tried to climb onto the sink to wash her hands and fell. The three-year-old insisted she was too hurt to walk and Mom couldn't carry the baby and the three-year-old out at once. I was just helping, so no, unfortunately, they weren't handing out babies in there. If they had been, I would have taken one. Or two or three…"

"Wow, you really do want kids," he muttered as their waiter arrived with the leather folder containing the bill and, it turned out, Gideon's credit card.

"This was supposed to be my treat," Jani protested when it became obvious that he'd paid the bill.

"You can treat me to the community center," he said as he signed and took his copy of the credit card slip. "I feel like a walk—are you up for it?"

That surprised Jani. As always, he'd been cool and aloof at the start of this evening, then all-business during the meal they'd eaten while going over the proposal and the cost estimates for the community center. It truly had been nothing more than the business dinner she'd claimed it was to her cousins.

But an after-dinner walk? That seemed to go beyond business.

"It's not too cold but there's that light snow that just started falling." Gideon pointed at the window beside their table. "Seems like a perfect night for a short winter stroll, but if that doesn't appeal to you…"

It definitely appealed to her…

"No, that does sound good," she insisted, glad now that she'd opted for the slacks and sweater. And shoes that she could easily walk in.

Jani slid the file folder with the paperwork into her large purse. While she did, Gideon put on his coat—a dressy leather jacket that he wore over a fisherman's turtleneck sweater and cocoa-colored slacks.

Then he took Jani's knee-length, red wool coat before she could reach it and held it open for her to slip into.

As she did, a sense of the power of this big man standing so close came over her. She had the image of resting her back against his chest and having his arms envelop her the way the red wool did.

Where did that *come from?*

She yanked herself out of that bit of involuntary and unwanted reverie, muttered a simple "Thanks" and stepped away from him to button the coat from top to bottom as she commanded her fickle mind to behave.

She wrapped an angora scarf that went with her sweater twice around her neck—nearly strangling herself as punishment—then took matching gloves from her coat pockets and put them on.

When they got outside, Gideon seemed to have something in mind because he guided her across First Avenue down Milwaukee, and then turned right.

They passed by small boutique shops that were all closed at that hour, and a few restaurants and bars. But then they wandered away from the upscale section into a quieter, less affluent area.

When Colorado Boulevard came into sight a few blocks ahead of them Gideon stopped and pointed to the end where traffic was racing by.

"See that place down on the corner?"

"The dive that just seems to be named Bar?" Jani asked of the old, run-down white building with nothing more than a neon sign flashing the word.

"Uh-huh. That's where my great-grandfather ended up after Lakeview chased him out as their mayor."

Uh-oh. Apparently this wasn't merely an after-dinner stroll....

Jani could tell even from a distance that the bar wasn't anywhere she'd want to spend time.

"You mentioned that Lakeview ran your great-grandfather out of town but you didn't say how…"

"He became a pariah in Lakeview when it was clear that the promises he'd made on H.J.'s behalf weren't coming through. The way Lakeview's government was set up at the time, the city council had the power. The mayor was the head of the city council but had only one vote—"

"Like it is on the Camden board."

"Right. The mayor presided over the council, had some other minor responsibilities, and of course he was the ceremonial head of the community, but it didn't take much to shut him out—"

"Which was what happened?"

"Which was what happened. No one on the council would speak to him, or listen to anything he had to say. They made sure his vote was always overridden. He was told not to attend the ceremonial things that were the mayor's usual duties. And for all intents and purposes, he became the invisible mayor until he was finally forced to resign—basically in shame."

"That's not good…" Jani said quietly, unsure what else to say. "Is that when he 'ended up' at the bar? And did he buy it or work there or…" She feared the worst, that maybe his great-grandfather had ended up a drunken fixture there.

"While he was struggling as the invisible mayor and trying to convince people that he was *not* in H. J. Camden's pocket, his business in the private sector also went under—"

"What was his business?" Jani asked, hating what she was hearing even though Gideon was telling her this matter-of-factly and without the animosity he'd exhibited before.

"He owned Franklin Thatcher Insurance. He'd built it from the ground up, and it was doing well—he was a leading businessman, which was part of what helped him win his mayor's seat in the first place. But a majority of his clients were in Lakeview and after the Camden warehouses and factories were all that came of the deal with H. J. Camden, there was a boycott on Franklin Thatcher Insurance. The agency went under. Then his house was torched—"

"No…" Jani said, flinching from that thought. She dug her hands into her pockets and shrugged deeper into her coat and scarf as it suddenly seemed to get colder.

"Yep, somebody burned down his house. At least they made sure my great-grandparents and my grandfather weren't in it at the time, but they lost everything. Literally. They ended up with the clothes on their backs and a car that had been smashed all to hell with baseball bats during an attack of vandals a couple of nights earlier. There wasn't a lot of effort put into finding out who did it all."

"Oh, Gideon…" Jani said with heartfelt sympathy.

"That was when they ended up here—my great-grandfather got a job mopping up, emptying the trash, general maintenance. My great-grandmother made sandwiches to sell with her pickles and deviled eggs as bar food, and the owner let my great-grandparents and my grandfather live in the two-room apartment above the bar because he felt sorry for them."

It just got worse and worse; Jani was huddled inside of her coat as much from the cold as from shame.

But when Gideon noticed, he only thought that she was cold and suggested they head back.

"So your grandfather grew up in two rooms over that bar?" Jani asked as they retraced their steps. She didn't want to hear any more but she knew she had to and, since Gideon seemed to be in a talkative mood, she also knew she had to pursue it. Plus, despite the subject matter, he wasn't displaying any hostility and that helped.

"On the first round, my grandfather was here for only four years—he was twelve when they left Lakeview. It was tough on him, too. He'd had his friends turn on him, literally throw rocks at him, beat him up—the stuff of twelve-year-olds taking out their parents' frustrations on the son of the man they held responsible for misleading them. My grandfather didn't adjust well to his new school, he didn't try to make new friends, and when he was sixteen he dropped out, and lied about his age to join the army."

"How did that work out for him?" Jani asked, hoping for the best but not expecting it.

"He didn't rise through the ranks. He apparently had a chip on his shoulder and was in trouble quite a bit for insubordination."

"He had a lot of anger," Jani guessed. Then she added quickly, "Not that he didn't have reason..."

But this time Gideon didn't jump on that the way he might have in previous encounters. Instead he merely confirmed that, yes, his grandfather had been an angry man his entire life.

Then he said, "When my grandfather got out of the service he ended up right back at the bar again, tending bar rather than sweeping up—I guess that was an improvement."

"But it's where he spent his life, too?"

"My whole family had trouble getting away from that place. It was like it had a hold on them. Or maybe, after Lakeview, they just didn't have the courage to move too far from the hole they'd hidden in," Gideon mused. "The anger and hatred that drove my great-grandparents and my grandfather out of Lakeview followed them for a few years, but they were still so beaten down by it long after the Thatcher name didn't mean anything to anyone outside of Lakeview."

"Did you know your great-grandparents?"

"I was little when they were around, I only remember them as frail, fearful old people. Furious really is what my grandfather was, right to his grave, furious and unhappy, and yeah, so beaten down by what had happened to him as a kid in Lakeview that he even passed on his defeatist attitude to my father—"

"Was your father raised around the bar, too?"

"Yeah. My grandmother was a regular patron—that's how she and my grandfather got together. It didn't make for the best connection. My grandfather married her when she got pregnant with my father but by the time my father was two, my grandmother had run off with some other guy and was never heard from again. My great-grandmother had died, there was just my great-grandfather, my grandfather, my two-year-old father and the bar—"

"Were they all still living in the apartment over it?" Jani asked, afraid of the answer.

"Yeah. My great-grandparents never left it. For my grandfather and my father there were a couple of moves into other places, but then money would get bad and they'd end up back there. It's where my father grew up."

Jani didn't know what to say about that but Gideon's tone let her know it wasn't something he was happy to report.

"Did your dad make it through school?" she asked.

"He got his high school diploma, but it didn't really matter. He was drinking before he ever graduated. He went to work bartending as soon as he was old enough, too. His greatest ambition was for him and my grandfather to buy the bar—"

"Did they?"

"Nah. They could never scrape up the money. My dad just stayed tending bar, doing it the same way his father did—pour a drink for the customer, pour one for themselves if they could get the customer to buy. My grandfather weathered the boozing better than my old man—my grandfather made it into his sixties before liver disease brought on by alcoholism killed him. My father only made it to forty-seven."

And all of it tracked back to what *her* great-grandfather had done…

"I'm so sorry..." Jani said, genuinely contrite. Then she asked another question she was dreading the answer to. "What about you? Did you grow up in that bar, too?"

"I started out there, but no," he answered without going into more detail. Instead he said, "I just thought that since we were this close, maybe you ought to see where the Thatchers landed post-Lakeview."

Landed and got stuck...

Jani and Gideon had reached the much more trendy stretch of the street again but were only about halfway back to the restaurant. They drew up to a cart set among a ring of heat lamps outside an ice cream parlor. Gourmet hot chocolate was being sold from the cart, and the cold January night—and a heavy helping of guilt—inspired Jani to say, "How about a little hot chocolate for the rest of the walk? You didn't let me buy you dinner, at least let me buy this."

He didn't argue, so they both warmed up under one of the lamps while cups of molten chocolate and cream were prepared for them.

When they were on their way again, sipping as they went, Jani decided to push a little and said, "So you started out at the bar but didn't grow up there?"

"My parents met there, too, but not because my mother was a barfly the way my grandmother was. My mother was a nurse's aide at the medical center when the main campus for the medical school was farther north on Colorado Boulevard. She got off work late one night and her car made it just far enough to die outside of the bar. The bar was open so she went in."

"And your dad was pouring drinks," Jani concluded.

"Right. He was only about a year into it by then— my mother said his drinking was in the early stages.

Anyway, he bought her a drink, flirted with her until closing, then went out to take a look at her car. They were married six months later. I was born ten months after that."

"And went home from the hospital to the apartment over the bar?"

"Yep," he said fatalistically. "My mother was young, she'd come from modest means herself, she wasn't too put off by it at first—"

"Were your great-grandfather and grandfather still living there, too?" Jani asked, finding it difficult to believe that a new bride was thrilled to live above that bar.

"No, they gave the place over to the newlyweds and rented a room in a boarding house within walking distance of the bar."

"So at least they had the apartment to themselves…" Jani said, trying to find a silver lining somewhere.

"Yeah. My father had told my mother that he was going to own the bar eventually, that they just needed to live there long enough to save some money. I was about four by the time she realized that was more my father's pipe dream than anything that would ever actually happen. And his drinking had gotten worse and worse on top of it."

"She left him?"

"No, but her goal had become to put some distance between him and that bar. He wouldn't quit his job there—he was still swearing he was going to buy the place, that it was his future. But she at least forced him to make a move out of the apartment above it and told him he could only spend time there when he was working."

"He agreed to that?" Jani asked, sipping the steaming drink.

"Well, he agreed, but he didn't abide by the agreement. They got a little apartment a few blocks away, and my great-grandfather and grandfather moved back into the one over the bar. But my father still spent his off hours there. My parents were divorced by the time I was six. Which was when my mother and I had to move in with her mother."

Gideon's frown when he said that was very dark, leading Jani to assume it hadn't been a positive experience.

"You didn't like your maternal grandmother?"

His eyebrows arched. "Oh, sure, I liked her. But my grandfather on that side had died before I was born and my grandmother wasn't well. The living arrangement was really just a necessity all the way around. Financially, and so that my grandmother had the care she needed, and in order for me to have an adult around when my mother had to work night shifts. But my poor mother worked as a nurse's aide, then came home to take care of my grandmother's failing health. And me and everything else. Plus there were only two bedrooms in my grandmother's house, so I grew up sleeping on the couch—"

"The whole time you were growing up, you didn't have a *bedroom?*"

"Or a bed," he said with a humorless laugh.

"Was the couch a fold-out?"

"Nope, just a couch. I did put sheets and blankets on it every night. And I had a pillow—"

"But it wasn't even a fold-out couch," Jani lamented.

"How long was it before you got a bedroom. And a bed?"

"When my grandmother died. I was sixteen. Then my mother took her room and I got my mother's room. And a new mattress, which was a treat."

"But still, you slept for *ten years* on a couch?" Jani said in dismay. "Finances were that bad?"

"I loved my dad, he was good-hearted. But he drank everything he earned. My mom didn't make much as a nurse's aide, so yeah, finances were always bad. I worked wherever I could—mowing lawns, shoveling snow, anything for a few bucks until I was old enough to get a formal job along with the odd jobs. But even then it was only after school and on weekends—I'd seen enough, I was getting an education come hell or high water."

"Which you did—high school, college *and* a graduate degree," Jani said, her admiration for him mounting along with the guilt she was feeling.

"Is your mom still around?" she asked, hoping that the woman had at least benefited from Gideon's success.

But he shook his head sadly. "She died of a massive coronary three months before I graduated with my bachelor's degree. Six months after my dad had died. At barely twenty-two I became all there was of the Thatchers or the Wadells—that was my mother's maiden name."

Jani closed her eyes and shook her head slowly back and forth as they crossed First Avenue, threw their empty cups in a trash can and returned to the restaurant parking lot.

She was grateful that Gideon hadn't shown any animosity or hostility tonight as he told her his family history. But now she also marveled at the fact that he'd told the entire story without a drop of self-pity, either.

It was impossible not to be impressed by him. And not only because he was tall and lean and broad-shouldered and drop-dead gorgeous, or because he exuded self-assurance in every step. It was impossible for her not to look at him and see how far he'd come, on his own, to achieve all he'd achieved. To be the man he seemed to be. A man who wanted some honor and dignity restored to his family name. Honor and dignity that her own great-grandfather had stolen...

"It's hard not to think about how different things might have been if Franklin Thatcher had gone on being mayor of Lakeview and owning his insurance agency, isn't it?" Jani asked.

"Sure. Over the years I've done a lot of that. After hearing as much as I did about the glory days when my great-grandfather was mayor, when my grandfather was king of the hill because he was the mayor's son, after hearing as much as I did about what might have been, I had my own fantasies—"

"Like what?" Jani asked, wondering if the Camdens might still be able to help make those fantasies a reality.

"I'd imagine that we lived in the suburban dream community my great-grandfather might have built. That I was important because I was a Thatcher—the great-grandson of the mayor," he said, smiling slightly at the flourish he used with that title. "In my head I'd make my grandfather a businessman—selling insurance at the agency he'd taken over. I'd imagine that my father wasn't a slave to a glass, that he and my mother stayed together out in the burbs where he probably sold insurance, too—"

"And I'm sure you'd picture yourself with your own bedroom. Your own bed…" Jani said, her heart breaking for the young Gideon, that heartbreak echoing in the softness of her voice. "You *do* have a bed now, don't you?"

Something about that made him laugh as he leaned against her car, bringing him slightly closer in front of her. Enough so that Jani could feel a little of the heat radiating from him and smell the faint scent of a clean, crisp cologne that she liked. A lot…

"You're making me feel guilty," Gideon said.

"*I'm* making you feel guilty?" Jani asked in astonishment.

"You look like a deer I've caught in my headlights. You really didn't have any—*any*—idea of what H. J. Camden brought about, did you?"

"Until very recently, all we knew was that we have factories and warehouses in Lakeview that were built there in the fifties."

Gideon's eyebrows arched and he shook his head. "You're kidding?"

"I'm not. Business and family were always completely separate for H.J., for my grandfather and my father and my uncle, too. My generation has taken over and we're committed to doing things fairly, doing things the right way. But as far as what went on in the building of Camden Inc.? We didn't know anything about that. Not even my grandmother knew anything about it."

"Until recently…" Gideon repeated her earlier words.

Jani merely shrugged; she couldn't go into the discovery of H.J.'s journals and all they'd revealed.

Gideon cocked his head. "So you really were removed from—"

"Everything to do with the business until I was grown up and by then what was done was—"

"History to you."

"But what was just history to me had a wide ripple effect for you."

"Which is why I get to pin the blame on you, to hold you responsible. But when I do, you can't look so shocked—let's make that a ground rule," he joked, laughing again.

He'd joked. He'd laughed. Gideon Thatcher had a sense of humor. A sense of humor that Jani appreciated. And reveled in when it caused the transformation of his oh-so-handsome face, when levity drew creases at the corners of those green eyes, and his chiseled features grew all the more striking...

"I'm sorry for being shocked," Jani joked in return. "Next time I'll try to be callous and tough and—"

"And you'll say 'Ah, suck it up, Thatcher' so I can sling some more mud your way with a clean conscience rather than feel guilty for laying it all on you?"

"I don't know about being callous enough to tell you to suck it up—you had to sleep on your grandmother's couch for ten years," Jani said. Then, in all seriousness, she added, "But I really am sorry for what your family went through because of what H.J. did."

Gideon was looking intently at her, into her eyes, and maybe something he saw there convinced him of her sincerity because he merely nodded, accepting her apology.

"And someday you'll tell me your side of it," he reminded, for once not defensively, actually sounding as if he might be opening the door to her. Just a crack.

"Someday..." Jani said with less conviction than

usual. What she had to say in H.J.'s defense now seemed more feeble than it had to her before.

And then, as they stood there peering at one another, something seemed to change between them. Jani wasn't sure what it was, but she felt some of the tension that had always been around them fall away. Suddenly it was as if they were just two people standing beside her car after spending the evening together.

He smiled again. The smile was more open than she'd seen from him before and laced with a hint of mischief. "But if you really are sorry, I'll tell you one thing you can do for Lakeview—"

"Besides the community center?" Jani asked.

"If you seriously want to make up for what went on way back when, you can help me man one of the flea market booths tomorrow. There's a fund-raising bazaar in the park around Shones Lake. I'm signed on for the library booth to sell old books. All the money goes into the city coffers for the redevelopment. Or is that more down and dirty than you're willing to go?"

He was challenging her again but there was a hint of playfulness to it tonight.

"Believe me, I'm feeling so guilty that I'd agree to build the booths with my own two hands, and then buy all the books myself."

"Guilt—I can work with that," he said as if she were giving him ideas. "Does that mean I can count on you?"

"Just tell me when to be wherever I need to be."

"We're taking up a big section of the park—you won't be able to miss us. I'll be in the booth closest to the library—less distance to haul books. The bazaar and flea market opens at nine. Set up's at eight. Dress for work. Don't wear heels."

They both glanced down at her shoes and when they looked back up at each other he seemed to be just a little nearer.

"I do have conservative shoes," she assured him.

"You'll be on your feet all day, so wear them."

"Yes, sir!" she said with mock obedience that made him smile again.

Oh, but she loved to see that smile…

She realized then that regardless of the intense emotions that had been raised by Gideon's revelations about his family history, she'd still had a good time with him.

And maybe he hadn't had such a bad time with her, because he was studying her with a new, softer expression that told her the tension between them really was gone. At least for the moment.

Then, Gideon leaned forward and kissed her, shocking her even more than anything she'd learned tonight.

The lightest press of his lips to hers and it was over before she could even tilt her head up. But still, it was a kiss. On the lips.

He drew away as if it had taken him by surprise, too.

After a moment of that surprise flitting across his expression, he acted as if it hadn't happened.

Maybe because he wished it hadn't?

"So. Tomorrow at the park. Bright and early. If you dare," he said as he pushed away from her car and headed for his.

"Thanks for dinner," Jani belatedly called after him.

"Thanks for the hot chocolate," he called back as if not to be outdone, the sexy swagger of his walk making Jani slow to unlock her car door and get behind the wheel.

As she drove home, she still felt ashamed of the pain her family had caused his.

But somehow her thoughts began to turn more to the man who had risen from the ashes of his own family, and that caused her to think less and less about long ago and more about the recent past.

About that kiss.

Gideon Thatcher had *kissed* her....

And even though it hadn't really been anything, it still felt like something to her.

Something she wanted to try again...

Chapter Six

"Whoa! Buddy! That couldn't have felt good!"

Jani had glanced up from putting money in the library booth's cash box just in time to see a little boy fall flat on his face directly in front of their tented area, provoking Gideon's comment. He rushed out of the booth and went to the child.

It was Thorpe Armbruster, the four-year-old son of Lakeview councilwoman Amanda Armbruster, who was manning the Lakeview flea market's popcorn booth.

They couldn't have asked for a nicer January day for the flea market—it was sunny and fifty-two degrees—and Thorpe had spent most of the day visiting many of the booths under the watchful eye of his mother. But he seemed to have developed a particular fondness for Gideon because his trips since lunchtime had been to the book booth alone.

"I wuz bringin' you popcorn..." the little boy lamented, working to fight tears as Gideon helped him get on his feet. "I spilled it."

"That's okay. The birds and squirrels will take care of the popcorn."

After giving the child a quick once-over Gideon called to the councilwoman, "He's all right." Then, to distract Thorpe, Gideon said, "I knew someone who needed a particular book read to her every night before bed and sometimes when she didn't feel good or got hurt like you just did. Want to see it, or do you want to get back to your mom?"

"Wanna see it," the child said, still blinking back tears.

"It's about a bunch of bears—I think you'll like it."

The bear book...

Jani had arrived at the flea market at 8:00 a.m. sharp. Gideon was just getting out of his car when she'd pulled into the lot and had not disguised his shock that she'd come to pitch in.

The booths—some of them small, others larger and shaded by tent canopies—had already been set up when they'd arrived, but Jani had helped Gideon tote boxes of books from the library and they'd been working together ever since.

She'd seen him stall over the bear picture book when they'd unpacked it and thought maybe it was a book he'd remembered from his childhood. But apparently that wasn't the case, and now Jani's curiosity was sparked.

"Here it is," he said when he'd located it on the table that held books for kids.

Jani watched as he got the little boy interested in the book. It was only a matter of minutes before the blond child with the thick glasses seemed to have forgotten all about his fall, and Jani catalogued the technique for use when she had a child of her own to deal with.

But by then taking note of how Gideon dealt with kids was something she'd been doing for a while. In fact she'd found reason to do it each time Thorpe visited the book booth and Gideon had had any exchange with him.

The man was a natural with children, which surprised Jani as much as her early arrival had surprised him. He didn't go overboard with Thorpe. He never talked down to the four-year-old. He didn't try to be cool or cutesy or silly with him, he just treated him like anyone else, patiently answering his questions and listening to what Thorpe had to say. And all as calmly as if he were an old hand at it.

"Can I have this book?" Thorpe asked.

"If it's all right with your mom. Why don't you show it to her, tell her it's my treat. But don't run."

Thorpe took the book and walked with purpose to the popcorn booth.

After listening to her son for a moment, the councilwoman waved her approval and Gideon took his wallet from the back pocket of his jeans to put a dollar in the cash box.

"Please don't tell me that whoever it was you read that book to every night before bed was your last girlfriend," Jani teased him, fishing for information in the process.

As the day had progressed they'd both relaxed more than they had at any other time they'd been together. She'd come to see that Gideon Thatcher actually had a fun—and funny—side. A side that was a little ornery and mischievous and far more lighthearted than she would ever have imagined. A side that had allowed for joking and teasing. And maybe just a little flirting, too.

It had made the time go faster—and far more pleasantly—for Jani, even though she did keep telling herself that flirting was probably not a good idea.

Despite the fact that her comment just now had clearly been a joke, Gideon's smile in response wasn't as open or relaxed as what she'd come to expect from him today. Instead it was bittersweet, and Jani knew instantly that she'd somehow struck a nerve again.

"I read the bear book over and over again to my daughter," he said stiffly.

Jani very nearly dropped the notebook where she'd just entered the title of the bear book and the amount Gideon had paid for it.

His *daughter?*

"You said you were divorced. I didn't realize you had kids," Jani said without any levity at all.

"I don't," he answered in a clipped tone that left her more curious than she had been before.

"You read the bear book to your daughter, but you don't have kids..." Jani said, trying to figure out the riddle of that.

But he acted as if he hadn't heard her and instead went to straighten the table of books farthest away from her.

Oh, this can't be good, Jani thought.

But before she knew how—or if—she should pursue the subject, she thought she heard her grandmother's voice in the distance, saying, "There she is! Over at that one."

Turning away from the sight of Gideon's broad back in the thick gray wool sweater he was wearing with jeans, Jani looked out into the crowd of shoppers milling around the booths. She sincerely hoped her ears had been deceiving her, but they hadn't. GiGi was indeed making her way in Jani's direction.

She'd spoken to her grandmother after leaving Gideon the night before and told GiGi all she'd learned about the Thatchers. She'd also told her grandmother that she had agreed to work the flea market today. The elderly woman had given no clue that she might show up.

But there she was suddenly, accompanied by the man who had become her constant companion since the two high school sweethearts had reconnected in October.

"Hi, honey!" her grandmother greeted her when the two older people arrived at the book booth.

At seventy-five years old, they were still both in robustly good health, despite carrying a few more pounds than they should have been on their short frames. GiGi's blue eyes still sparkled with vigor, and she looked sporty with her salt-and-pepper hair curled around her face. And Jonah's shock of thick white hair and ruddy cheeks gave him the overall appearance of a spry, beardless Santa.

"GiGi," Jani said. "I didn't know you were coming."

She also didn't know how her grandmother being there would go over with Gideon. Especially since his darker side had made a reappearance.

Plus there was the noteworthy fact that in all the introductions he'd made today, he'd never once used Jani's last name. No one was aware that she was a Camden, and Jani knew that was how he wanted it. That he didn't want his name connected in any way with the Camden name, particularly in Lakeview.

Jani had merely accepted that. But now here GiGi was, and Jani wondered if she would open a can of worms.

"Jonah and I spent the day together and now we're going back to Arden to have dinner at his house with Cade and Nati. Since we were driving right by here on the way, I asked him to stop," GiGi explained.

Cade had met his fiancée, Nati, on his mission to make amends for past Camden misdeeds. It's what had brought GiGi back together with Jonah Morrison, who was Nati's grandfather. Now GiGi was spending more time in Arden, a suburb west of both Denver and Lakeview where Jonah lived.

"Hello! You must be Gideon Thatcher. I'm Jani's grandmother," GiGi called, looking beyond Jani to Gideon, who had not rushed to join them.

Jani was glad her grandmother hadn't uttered their last name but there was still a moment of extreme tension for her when she wasn't sure what was going to happen, when she worried what Gideon's reaction might be, when she just hoped he didn't mistreat her grandmother because if he did, there would be no turning back as far as Jani was concerned.

But after that moment of tension, Gideon joined them.

"Hi," he said, still sounding stiff but courteous nonetheless.

"This is my friend Jonah Morrison." GiGi went on with the introductions since Jani was too nervous to make them herself. "Jonah, this is Gideon Thatcher. And you can call me GiGi, Mr. Thatcher—everyone does."

"Gideon," Gideon said perfunctorily, shaking Jonah's hand.

"My granddaughter speaks well of you, Gideon," GiGi said then.

"Really…" One of Gideon's eyebrows arched dubiously as he angled a glance at Jani.

"Well, you know, maybe not so much at first," GiGi admitted with a laugh, causing Jani to grimace at the revelation. "I understand the start was a little rocky. But that doesn't mean things have to stay that way, does it, Jonah?" She nudged her companion with an elbow and sent him a sly glance.

"Nope. Sometimes the best things are at the end of rocky roads," Jonah said with a clearly lascivious wink.

Jani caught Gideon's eye, made a face and shook her head helplessly.

Something about her discomfort seemed to amuse him because he cracked the barest of smiles before GiGi drew his attention again.

"Anyway, I just wanted to stop and tell you how happy I am that you've agreed to let us help to honor Franklin Thatcher," GiGi confided to Gideon in a lowered voice that couldn't be heard by anyone else. Jani realized that her grandmother had not lost sight of Gideon's position in the community and was trying to stay anonymous.

Gideon merely raised his chin in response to what her grandmother had said, and Jani saw a muscle flex in his jaw that let her know he wasn't entirely happy with her grandmother's endorsement.

"I asked everyone to look over things today—we got your proposal and the cost estimates from Jani early this morning. We're all fine with it and I wanted to give you the go-ahead. Do you like pot roast?"

The speed with which GiGi had changed the subject startled both Jani and Gideon.

"Do I like pot roast?" he repeated.

"Pot roast, potatoes, carrots, little pearl onions, gravy, salad—the works."

"Yes…" Gideon said, obviously confused by the direction this had taken. But Jani was beginning to understand. And worry again.

"I do Sunday dinner every week," the enthusiastic GiGi announced. "Family. Friends. Family of friends. Friends of friends—it's a friendly free-for-all and tomorrow we're having pot roast. Come, I'll feed you and give you a check so you can put the wheels into motion on this thing."

"Oh, I don't—"

"No, no, no, I never take no for an answer to my Sunday dinners. You'll be Jani's and my special guest, you'll come away with a full stomach and a check to make it worth your while." She pointed an index finger at Jani. "Don't let him out of it! I'll see you both tomorrow. Good to meet you, Gideon." And just like that, she and Jonah left, with Jonah merely waving his goodbye as he went.

"Soo… That's my grandmother—sometimes she can be a bit of a whirlwind…" Jani said softly as they watched the older couple disappear back into the crowd. "Thanks for being polite to her." Although GiGi hadn't given him much of an opportunity to get a word in edgewise.

"Takes-no-prisoners kind of lady," Gideon observed. But without animosity. Jani was thankful for that.

"She's a force to be reckoned with. But we all love her dearly and while you might not agree since she's just steamrolled you, her strong will is generally a good thing."

His eyebrows arched again and Jani could see he likely didn't agree.

"Really," she insisted. "If it hadn't been for that strong will this family would have fallen apart, and I don't know what might have happened to us all."

"Why is that? I haven't kept up with the latest Camden news, but I thought H.J. was captain of the ship."

"H.J. was captain of the business ship. But when it comes to the family, GiGi has been at that helm. It was GiGi who even took care of H.J.—he went to live with her and my grandfather when he had his heart attack and decided to retire, when he really wasn't doing well on his own after my great-grandmother died. And it was GiGi who was home taking care of him because he'd hurt his back when the plane crash took the rest of the family—"

"The plane crash…" The words seemed to spark a memory for Gideon. "I was just a kid but I do remember that there was a plane crash—"

"I'm sure your family was among those who thought it was comeuppance," Jani said, imagining the Thatchers taking some satisfaction from tragedy befalling the Camdens.

Gideon didn't deny that. "My family was betting someone had blown the plane up—that's why I remember it. It seemed like a movie or something bigger than life."

"There's always been the suspicion that foul play

was involved, yes," Jani confirmed. "But there wasn't enough wreckage left to prove it."

"And who all went down in the crash?"

"Everyone but GiGi, H.J. and the ten of us grand-children—"

"I didn't realize… So you were orphaned?" Gideon said with unmasked surprised.

"And GiGi was widowed. My parents, my aunt and uncle, my grandfather were on the plane. It was a family vacation that GiGi and H.J. missed at the last minute because of H.J.'s hurt back."

Light seemed to dawn in Gideon. "That's why you said something before about H.J. helping your grand-mother raise you all—when you said that I wasn't actu-ally thinking that she raised you *without* your parents being around. I was just thinking that it was…I don't know, a family affair to raise the kids, I guess. But you meant it literally—your grandmother and H.J. really did raise you?"

"From the time I was six. The triplets—my cous-ins—were six, too. We're the youngest. From there the ages varied up to eleven."

"She took on ten kids, eleven and under?"

"Yep. With the help of H.J. and Margaret and Louie—Margaret and Louie have worked for GiGi for-ever, long enough to be part of the family. When the ten of us moved in, it was understood that we answered to Margaret and Louie every bit as much as we answered to GiGi and H.J."

"And you were just six… How was that for you? I don't suppose you cared a lot about being a Camden or having the world at your disposal then. You were prob-ably just a scared little kid…"

"Yeah," Jani said because it was true. "A lot of it is sort of a blur—I remember being taken to GiGi's house with my brothers, that my cousins were all there, too. I remember that something didn't feel right, even though we were all at GiGi's often enough that it shouldn't have raised any red flags. I remember H.J. sitting in a chair, looking really old and sick—"

"His back was hurt," Gideon pointed out.

"But I'd seen him since his back had been hurt and this was different. Margaret and Louie were there, too, and Margaret stayed really close to GiGi—for support, I'm sure. But at the time I was wondering why Margaret and GiGi were holding hands. And I remember a box of tissues on the coffee table—we were all in the living room and there weren't ever tissues in the living room…"

Jani laughed a sad little laugh. "It's weird the things that stick with you. Then GiGi told us what had happened. She had to explain to the triplets and me that it meant our mothers and fathers wouldn't ever be coming home—"

"At six you didn't have much of a concept of death."

"None. GiGi sort of bucked up then, told us we were all moving there to live with her, that we were all still family and would go on as a family—with Margaret's and Louie's help. The funerals, the time after that isn't clear in my mind. Then all of our stuff showed up at GiGi's. I shared a room with my two girl cousins, Lindie and Livi, who are also two of the three triplets. Sharing a room was new for me, I'd had my own room until then. The seven boy cousins were split up into two other rooms, and that was it—we all lived together from them on."

"Happily?"

"Just like any other family. At first things were a mess and I didn't help matters."

"What did you do?"

"Everyone would probably disagree with this, but it seemed to me that I had the most problems adjusting. Lindie and Livi had always had each other, had shared a room, and they were sort of their own little support system, while I was the third wheel. The boys—my brothers and my other cousins—were all…boys. They did a lot of keeping a stiff upper lip, not showing much, telling me not to be such a baby when I did get upset. So I felt kind of…alone, as strange as that may sound when I was living in a house with nine other kids and four adults."

"You were still just six years old and pretty much odd man out," Gideon summarized sympathetically.

"And dealing with the death of the two most important people in my life. I acted out—I was basically just a brat. I had nightmares and my screaming would wake up the whole house. And then there was the sleep-walking—"

"You're a sleepwalker?"

"Not since I was about eight. But until then, going to sleep in my bed didn't mean that was where they'd find me in the morning. Or where I'd wake up."

His smile was sad and sympathetic, but amused, too. "Where *did* you wake up?"

"In bathtubs, under beds, in the attic, outside. The weirdest was in the clothes dryer—Margaret found me there one morning. It was an industrial-sized dryer and luckily I hadn't closed the door or I guess I might have suffocated. Poor GiGi—that one really scared her. She didn't know what to do with me. For everyone else, talking to a therapist was optional, but I *had* to. Which I hated—"

"But did it help?"

"I think it just helped GiGi feel like she was doing *something* when she didn't know what else to do. And after the dryer incident she had an alarm put on our bedroom door. It only sounded in her room if the door was opened, so everyone else could sleep, but she'd know if I was on the move and coax me back to bed before I got into any trouble."

"Smart."

"Yep, GiGi is that, too," Jani said proudly.

"So when did everything calm down? Or did it?"

"It did. Eventually it got as calm as a house with that many kids in it ever gets. But I think it took about two years. Until then the best I can say is that there were good days and bad. For all of us, really, even though I was mostly figuring it was me who had it bad." Jani laughed at her own self-centeredness.

"When did H.J. start impressing upon you all that you had a responsibility to take over the company— when you were just a little kid or—?"

"Pretty soon after we started living with him and GiGi. He had to come out of retirement and go back to running the business right after the plane crash— everyone who had been doing it was gone. But he was eighty-eight at the time."

"Wow, and he was still *able* to go back to work?"

"His mind was sharp until a few months before he died, so that wasn't a problem. Physically it was more difficult for him, so he established a group of people he trusted to do most of his legwork. He also enlisted those same people to take care of things if and when something happened to him, to mentor all of us until we could handle the business ourselves."

"Did you have a choice?"

There was some criticism in Gideon's question that H.J. didn't deserve, and Jani defended her grandfather. "It wasn't easy on him, either. He'd lost his only son, his two grandsons—not only his family, but the people he'd relied on in business, too. He was eighty-eight and he had to go back to work. GiGi and H.J. just did what they had to do for all of us. Maybe, because of how things ended up, we fell into more responsibilities than we might have had otherwise, but he did what he had to do."

Her voice had grown soft again as she finished, and when she glanced at Gideon, he was watching her with a new sort of expression on his face that made her think he might be torn, that maybe he was seeing something for the first time that he didn't really want to see.

"I suppose pain and suffering and loss are the same no matter who you are," he said then.

"It isn't easy for anybody to send their family off on a vacation and just have them not come back."

"No, I suppose not," he conceded.

"But," Jani continued, "we were also lucky to have each other. Lucky to have GiGi and a place to go. A place where we could all go together. And someone who was willing to take on ten of us at the same time she was dealing with her own grief and caring for her aging father-in-law."

"Ten kids…" Gideon marveled. "I can't imagine that. One is more of a handful than you think it's going to be…."

"GiGi has a big house but ten kids is still a lot, yeah."

"And did you stay the odd man out the whole time?"

"No, eventually we all settled in and found our way. We actually became one really solid family. Lindie, Livi and I are like sisters. And for better or worse, my boy cousins became more like brothers so I ended up with seven brothers instead of three."

"That's a lot," Gideon marveled.

"Yeah, you have never really been tortured until you've had your face held in a bag filled with the smelly socks of seven teenage boys."

"Oh, that would be bad!" Gideon commiserated even as he laughed.

At that moment the staff from the library came to help them box books and return what hadn't sold to the basement of the small old stone structure. Jani and Gideon had been so involved in talking that they hadn't noticed that the afternoon was ending—the crowd had dwindled and the rest of the booths were closing down.

That ended their conversation as they both went to work alongside the library staff.

When they were finished moving the books and folding and stacking the tables for the crew that was coming in to break down the flea market, Gideon walked Jani to the parking lot in the waning light.

"Busy tonight?" he asked casually.

"Only with cleaning a day's worth of old book dust and the great outdoors off my body and out of my hair," she answered.

"How about if after that, you come over to my place and I fix you dinner?"

That caught Jani off guard. They'd reached her car and she felt sure that her surprise showed in her expression when she looked up at Gideon's face to see if he was serious. "You're inviting me to dinner? At your place?"

He smiled as if he'd known all along how she would take that. "I am," he confirmed. "You worked hard today, you've worked hard every time you've come up against my grudge stuff—seems like that should have earned you something in return. Plus, picturing the six-year-old girl you were, sleepwalking and ending up in a dryer...I know I've been giving you a lot of flak and you've been taking it like a trouper, when maybe things haven't always been a picnic for you, either. I think maybe I need to cut back on the flak and give you just a little slack instead."

A concession...

"Wow," Jani said.

"Don't think I'm absolving that great-grandfather of yours of anything, though, because I'm not," he warned, the simple statement enough to bring a hint of rancor to his tone. Then the rancor was quickly replaced by kindness again. "But you...I'm gonna do my damnedest to separate the two of you some..."

Only some.

Still, some was more than none and Jani would take what she could get.

And going to his place, seeing how he lived, the private side of his life—that seemed like a part of this errand she was on.

Jani didn't hate the idea of cleaning up and spending the evening with him, either.

So she said, "You cook?"

"Nothing gourmet, but yeah, I can put together something pretty edible."

Jani pretended to think about it, then said, "Okay. Where do you live?"

"I'll text you the address and directions. I'm just outside of downtown, in the lofts that overlook the city."

"That's easy enough—I have a house in Cherry Creek."

"Say…eight o'clock? That'll give me time to shower and do some cooking."

"Okay," Jani agreed.

A gust of winter wind whipped around them just then, blowing Jani's hair across her face. She reached for it but Gideon beat her to it, hooking an index finger in the long strand to pull it away and just barely brushing her cheek in the process.

That scantest of touches sent a bit of a tingle through her. And when her hair was back in place and she looked up into Gideon's eyes, somehow he seemed nearer.

"Thanks," she said, wondering suddenly how he could have worked outside, in the open, all day long, and still look as good as he did. Because he *did* look good—all rugged and ruddy with just a little stubble of beard that only added to his handsome appeal.

Then, when it was the last thing she expected, he kissed her again.

Like the night before, it came out of nowhere.

But unlike the night before, this kiss wasn't over almost before it began. This kiss lingered. It was still only the lightest press of his mouth to hers, but it was enough for her to register it. To learn that his lips were warm and supple. And very, very adept. They were parted slightly, and she answered by raising her chin to him, parting her lips slightly, too, as she kissed him back…

But just for a moment before he ended the kiss. He

didn't hurry—instead it was a lazy sort of ending. He removed his lips from hers and gradually stood up straight as if he were coming out of a daze.

"I really did appreciate your help today," he said, implying that's what the kiss had been for.

"You're welcome…" Jani said in a soft voice, still under the influence of that kiss.

"And I'm sorry you lost your parents when you were just a little kid—I didn't say that before, but I'm saying it now. It was a raw deal of your own."

Jani merely shrugged her shoulders in response as his green eyes held hers in a moment that felt close and fleetingly intimate.

Then Gideon stepped back and it was business as usual. "I'll see you at eight."

"Can I bring something?"

"Wine, if you've got it. But don't make a special trip if you don't."

"Wine," Jani repeated to help herself remember.

"And come comfortable—this isn't… It's no big deal."

It isn't a date? Is that what he'd been going to say?

But of course it wasn't a date. If it was she'd have to refuse to go…

"Comfortable clothes, no big deal—got it," she repeated.

"See you then."

"At eight," Jani repeated as Gideon turned and headed for his car parked a few spots away from hers.

She got into her sedan then, thinking, *Dinner at eight. In comfortable clothes. No big deal…*

And not a date.

But he'd kissed her…

Twice now.

Kissing did not belong in any of this.

And she couldn't figure out why he'd done it.

Twice!

Or why today she'd kissed him back when she should have put a stop to it instead.

"Nothing this confusing can be good…" she muttered.

And yet nowhere in any of what she was feeling could she find regret for their kiss today.

No matter how hard she looked.

Or how much she knew it should be there.

Nope, no regret.

But what she did find was an alarming desire to have it happen again.

In spite of everything in her shouting that it shouldn't.

Chapter Seven

It isn't a date...
  It isn't a date...
  It isn't a date...

After paying close attention to every little detail when she'd showered, shampooed her hair and dressed for dinner at Gideon's place—and after racing to get there—Jani was still sitting in her car in the parking garage of his apartment building. It was five minutes until eight o'clock and she was resisting the urge to rush to the elevator. Forcing herself to remember that this was not a date.

Okay, yes she'd worn clothes she would have worn if this *was* a date. A casual date. She had on her best jeans—the ones she'd paid an arm and a leg for in Paris because no jeans had ever fit her the way these did. And she had on the cashmere sweater Lindie had given her for Christmas—it was black, just tight enough to show off her assets and it had the perfect, tall, neck-hugging turtleneck. She and Lindie and Livi all agreed that it made her look like some kind of sophisticated, sexy cat burglar.

She'd taken special pains with her hair, letting it air dry and fluffing it every twenty minutes until the waves were all just right, so that it fell around her face and shoulders exactly the way she liked it to.

The outdoor air had left her without a need for blush, but she'd used a tiny amount of eye shadow and liner to go with her usual mascara to accentuate her eye. And she'd applied her new pale mauve gloss.

The entire time she'd been primping, she'd continued to remind herself that this wasn't a date. That she had a job to do with Gideon, that that was the only reason she'd accepted his invitation tonight.

But she was well aware that in between those reminders, she'd also been thinking about his amazing green eyes and his chiseled features and his broad shoulders and his big hands and the softness of his lips when he'd kissed her....

And the fact that he'd kissed her.

And that she'd liked it...

"It isn't a date," she said out loud in the silence of her car. "This is going nowhere. I have a job to do, I'm doing it, when it's done this guy won't even exist for me anymore."

All true.

But it didn't help. Her stomach was still aflutter and she wanted to run—not walk—to the elevator that would get her to his place so she could see him again.

"Dial it back," she cautioned herself.

And then she used her secret weapon.

She closed her eyes, pictured the nursery she had planned. She pictured holding her baby in her arms. She felt the love she knew she would feel for it—boy or girl, it didn't matter. She saw herself at the park, watching children play and knowing one of them was hers. She saw herself as a mother. The mother she wanted to be more than anything.

And that did help.

Yes, she was increasingly more attracted to Gideon with every minute they spent together.

Yes, she thought he might be attracted to her in spite of who she was and the family history that was a thorn in his paw.

But that was all incidental. It was all just a brief blip on the radar and it would pass. In the end, amends would be made and they would go their separate ways.

And really, she reasoned, it was helpful that the icy wall had melted between them but it didn't have any greater meaning. Last night, she'd garnered a lot of information about Gideon's family and the effects H.J.'s actions had had on them. It was invaluable in her getting to know Gideon and how best to compensate the single living relative of Franklin Thatcher in order to make her family's amends. The fact that she wasn't dreading being with him to do the job was also a plus.

But all this didn't change the grand design of her life.

So she had to make sure that things with Gideon didn't heat up any more than they already had.

Which meant no more kissing.

But now that she knew the first time hadn't just been a fluke, that he'd been inclined to do it again, she told herself to just be on the alert so she could avoid it happening from now on.

It isn't a date. No kissing. Keep it simple. Do what you need to do, get it over with, move on...

Ground rules.

Jani took a deep breath, exhaled to clear her lungs, her mind, and to keep her focus where it needed to be—on the job she had to do, not on the man.

Then she got out of her car and headed for the elevator that would take her to the top floor of the seven-story building that housed Gideon's loft.

She was still feeling eager to see him. Much, much more eager than she wished she felt.

But she was also holding tight to her resolve.

"My steak was cooked perfectly, I love a baked potato with all the good stuff piled on, your special secret-of-the-house salad dressing is great and I would eat another roll but I couldn't get even one more bite down," Jani said, reviewing the meal that Gideon had prepared for her as they cleaned up together afterward.

"I'm glad you couldn't eat another bite because I'm afraid I dropped the ball on dessert," he said. "I stopped at my favorite bakery but they closed early today for some reason and I didn't have a back-up plan."

It was for the best, Jani decided. Dessert was more datelike, and after a meal accompanied by pleasant conversation with Gideon about the flea market, it was getting increasingly difficult to remember that this wasn't a date.

But in an attempt to keep on track, when the dishwasher was loaded, the counters wiped down and Gideon had poured them both a second glass of wine, Jani turned from the huge modern kitchen to look out into the rest of the wide-open space of his loft.

It definitely didn't speak of hardship, past or present. There were only two units that shared the entire top floor of the building, so nothing was compact in the space. The kitchen flowed into the dining room, which flowed into the living room and an area off that that Gideon was obviously using as a home office. The loft was high-ceilinged, stark and contemporary, furnished in expensive white leather, chrome and glass.

"This is a beautiful place," Jani commented.

"Thanks. I just bought it about six months ago. There are only two bedrooms, but that's all I need—a master suite and a guestroom. And each bedroom has its own bath."

Plus there was a powder room Jani had used to wash her hands before dinner.

She wandered across the space to the wall of windows that looked out from the living room over all of Denver. "And what a view!" she said.

Gideon joined her there. "It is great, isn't it?" he agreed, taking in the sight of the city lights while Jani's attention somehow shifted to his reflection in the glass.

It wasn't the first time tonight that she'd noticed how good he looked in jeans that were less faded than what he'd had on for the flea market. Jeans that fitted him well enough to have made her eyes roam on their own to his rear end at every opportunity.

It wasn't the first time tonight that she'd noticed how well his navy blue tweed Henley sweater hugged his shoulders and the expanse of his chest, either. Or that there was something very sexy about the look of his sleeves pushed to midforearm.

It wasn't the first time tonight that she'd noticed that his hair was shiny-clean and combed carelessly or that he'd shaved off the afternoon's stubble. Or that he smelled divine, too.

It was just the first time she'd noticed his male beauty reflected in the glass as if there were two of him, doubling the pleasure...

"...and I'm ten minutes from my office, from everything in the city," he was saying, still talking about the loft while she was thinking other things that she shouldn't have been thinking.

Jani reined in her thoughts and said, "I'm about ten minutes from my office and I bought my place six months ago, too. But I'm in a house not too far off Spear Boulevard."

"I was in a house before this."

"You didn't like it?"

"I did like it. But it needed to be sold—"

"It *needed* to be?" she said, concerned that financial problems might have been the cause.

He apparently realized what she was thinking because he said, "It wasn't that I couldn't afford it. It just had to be done."

"Divorce stuff?" Jani guessed, wondering if anything about his failed marriage could somehow be traced back to H.J.'s long-ago influence on his family and the course his life had taken as a result.

"Divorce stuff," Gideon confirmed, moving away from the window as if he were signaling that he wasn't willing to get into that subject.

Jani turned from the wall of glass, too.

"Sit down," he encouraged.

She did, going to the big leather sofa, where she sat near one end without hugging the arm too closely.

Gideon joined her there rather than taking either

of the less inviting suede director's chairs facing each other at opposite ends of the couch, sitting partially sideways.

Jani pivoted in his direction, closing even more of the distance between them.

But she tried not to notice this as she said, "If you liked your house, why didn't you want another one?" Because surely if he could afford a place like this, he could have afforded a house of his own after the divorce.

"I was going through big changes when I had to find a new place to live. I decided to embrace change completely."

Jani wasn't sure whether or not she was meant to probe it further. Deciding to err on the side of caution, she didn't. Instead, she glanced around again and said, "Well, it *is* a nice place."

"But you bought a house?" he said.

"I did. I thought it would be more kid-friendly."

"That was your primary concern?" he asked as if that seemed strange to him.

But of course it might seem strange because she didn't have any kids yet. She weighed whether or not to talk more about her determination to have a family. If this were a date, if he were a potential mate, she wouldn't because she'd be worried that it might scare him off this early. But this wasn't a date and her dating guard had no reason to be up, so she opted for honesty.

"A kid-friendly environment was definitely my primary concern," she admitted. "Down to the last detail— I bought a ranch-style so there aren't stairs. It's big but has a cozy, family feel. I made sure the bedrooms are close enough together that I'll be able to hear cries in the night. The nursery is light and airy and spacious enough for all the gear that goes with a baby. I have a big kitchen so we can cook together as a family the way GiGi always had all of us doing when I was growing up. There are great French doors that open onto a big patio—I can see myself looking out and watching a toddler on a tricycle riding around in circles. I have a yard that will fit playground equipment, but I'm also close to three different parks and not far from the zoo."

"And you're away from overly busy streets but near good schools?"

That sounded like the voice of experience...

"Also two of the things I looked for."

"That's a lot of kid-friendly, all right," he agreed. "And now you're all set?"

"I am. And I can't wait!"

He nodded stoically. "Be careful what you wish for..."

Jani laughed. "You make it sound so ominous."

He shrugged. "A kid will steal your heart more than you can ever imagine. It's actually a little scary. For me? Never again."

Because of the daughter he'd read the bear book to? The daughter he didn't still have in his life?

Initially Jani had assumed that he'd lost custody in the divorce and that's why he no longer saw her. But now she wondered if tragedy had taken his little girl from him. If maybe that tragedy had cost him his marriage, too.

She wanted to know. She needed to know in case it all had something to do with that bar his family had ended up in. Or related in some other convoluted way to the distant past, the Camden misdeeds she was trying to compensate him for. But she was suddenly too concerned with the weight of what might have happened to him to get openly nosy and decided that she should wait for him to seem willing to tell her more.

He proved he wasn't willing to talk about it yet by saying, "You really do have kids on the brain—I'd think you might have had enough of family after growing up surrounded by so much of it."

"It's the opposite actually. Once I got used to being part of such a big family it became really important to me. Then…" She wasn't going to tell him she only had one ovary or that it was smaller than normal, but she did say, "Well, when I was seventeen I found out I have lower-than-average odds of having kids of my own at all, and it became *more* important."

"Oh. I thought maybe you'd decided to have a kid on your own because you felt like you'd waited long enough for the right guy. Or maybe the wrong one left you thinking you weren't going to waste any more time with men."

So he'd given it some thought…

That made Jani smile. She opted for continuing in the vein of honesty. "Choice B," she said.

"So a bad experience with the wrong guy made you decide not to waste any more time with men?" he repeated.

"That might be a little harsh and make me sound like a man-hater, and I'm not," she hedged. "It's really about time—and how mine is slipping away. I can't risk wasting any more of it being on a hunt for a husband and then, you know, waiting for a relationship to develop and grow before *maybe* he asks me to marry him, and *maybe* we actually get to the altar."

"The wrong guy took forever to ask you to marry

him and then you still didn't get to the altar?" Gideon asked.

"It was more complicated than that..."

"And none of my business."

Again Jani thought that being open about herself might help lead him to be open with her—and ultimately help her achieve her goal. So she said, "No, it's okay. I don't have any secrets. I just lost four years believing in someone who disappointed me. He didn't actually take forever to propose—that happened after we'd been together a year."

"But getting to the altar?"

"Yeah, that never happened. Instead it was another three years of ups and downs. And with every down... Well, my hope for actually getting to the altar at all got a little less. Then terror sort of put it over the top for me and I was just relieved to get out of the relationship in one piece..."

Gideon's eyebrows arched toward his hairline. "Terror?" he echoed, setting his half-empty wineglass on one of two square, transparent glass coffee tables.

"Reggie—that's his name, Reginald Orton the Third," she said, affection and humor dusting her tone as she remembered how Reggie used to make jokes of saying the whole thing.

"You still don't hate the guy..."

"No," she admitted, though this time there was pity in her voice. "I loved Reggie and I wish him well—"

"Despite the terror?" Gideon said in confusion.

"Yeah, even despite that. He isn't a bad person, but he has a gambling problem. A really severe gambling problem."

Jani had had enough wine, too, so she put her own glass on the table nearest to her.

"Did you know he had a gambling problem going in?"

"No. Well, I did meet him at a casino night at the country club."

"That might have been a clue…"

"Less of one than you think. He was there as a guest of another member and he was just doing what everyone else was doing that night. And not to any excess—after we were introduced he paid more attention to me than to the games. So, no, I didn't know going in that he was a gambler. I heard along the way that he liked to have a good time, but sometimes that's just what a gambling addiction looks like until you see past the surface. It didn't really dawn on me until about a year and a half into our relationship that he had a serious—*serious*—issue."

"And you were already engaged by then."

"Right. Engaged, planning the wedding and how soon after that we could start a family."

"Just what you wanted."

"Just what I wanted," Jani said sadly, fighting her feelings as they cropped up.

"But the gambling was serious enough that you were terrorized by it?"

"Because of it, yes," Jani admitted, a shiver running through her even now at the memory, chasing away any lingering sadness or regret that things hadn't worked out with Reggie.

"Reggie truly isn't a bad guy," she felt compelled to say, not wanting to paint him as a villain. "He was actually a very sweet man. A lot of fun. Kind, thoughtful and personable—"

"You're giving me a complex," Gideon joked.

Was he somehow competing with her former fiancé?

"Don't worry, Reggie could never have made me the dinner you did," she joked back, thinking that Reggie's boyish good looks and slight build also couldn't hold a candle to the pure masculine beauty of Gideon. But she didn't say that. Instead she said, "All of Reggie's energies went into gambling. And hiding it."

"Nothing went into trying to stop it?"

Jani shrugged. "I think he tried. At least he made me think he did. After I realized that he had a problem, I learned everything I could about that kind of addiction, I went to support groups, I went to a counselor for advice on how to help him. How to save him from himself. How to fix him, I guess..."

"But sometimes you can't fight someone else's demons—whether it's drugs or booze or gambling or even cheating exes," Gideon said.

Jani wondered if he was speaking from experience and gave him a moment to expand on that, hoping he might.

He didn't, though. He went back to the subject at hand. "But *do* you think this Reggie guy wanted to be helped?"

"I don't know. He placed bets on everything you can imagine, things I didn't even know you could bet on. But he told me he wanted to stop. And, like I said, he gave the impression that he was trying—whether or not he was still doing a little gambling on the sly, I don't know. I know that for the two and a half years after I found out what was going on, there were times when I believed that he had cleaned up his act, that he was staying away from gambling. Times when there was no indication that he might be gambling so I'd let myself believe that the problem was behind us. Those were the ups, when I'd do some planning for the wedding and think it all might work out—"

"But?"

"But then something would happen to make me suspicious. I'd find something incriminating or I'd walk in on an unusual phone conversation that he'd be secretive about. Or I'd learn that he wasn't where he'd said he was going to be so I'd know he was sneaking around again. Or I'd just catch him taking money out of my purse…"

"He *stole* from you?"

"A little," Jani admitted, embarrassed by it. "Just cash. When I learned how bad his problem was, I did everything to make sure he couldn't get to anything more than that, but yes, he did take cash."

"Did the guy work for a living?"

"He'd started to sell luxury cars just before I met him. He told me it was only to keep himself busy—I knew his family had money, that he had lived on a trust fund until then. But the truth was that he'd gambled away the trust fund. He was essentially broke."

"And a liar."

"You learn that that goes along with addiction," Jani said fatalistically.

"And his rich family—what was going on with them when he was pilfering cash from you?"

"Again, I didn't know this at the start. At the start he did say he was on the outs with his family, but he acted like it was just a little family drama, nothing important. And he never filled me in. Later I found out that his family had gotten fed up with helping him pay his gambling debts. His relationship with them—parents and three siblings—improved when we got engaged…"

"Because they figured the Camden coffers are deep and they could bankroll him?"

"The possibility of him marrying me got him back in their good graces, so yes. It took me a while to figure out, but I believe they thought marrying a Camden was a way to pass Reggie off. Then they could go back to just being his family and leave supporting him and covering his gambling losses to me."

"And in return you could have had the kids you want…"

Jani sighed and once more felt some embarrassment when she confessed, "Yeah, I had that thought. Like I said, I did love Reggie and I know he loved me. And he was sweet and kind and he liked kids. He understood how badly I wanted them and he was ready to jump into that with me, too. So I had moments when I weighed the good against the bad and wondered if I should just accept that he had a problem and still try to have a life—and a family—with him."

"Your family wouldn't have let you do that, would they?"

"No one was in favor of it as time went on and they all got wind of Reggie's problems. They let me know they were worried. But we're not a family that turns its back because one of us does something the rest don't approve of or agree with. We just sort of wait it out and stay ready to pick up the pieces if it does go bad. Although by the end of this one, if I'd gone on with Reggie, I'm not sure if my family would have been able to just keep turning a blind eye."

"What about the terror part?" Gideon asked.

"It was last spring. I thought Reggie was doing okay but he was gambling and I just didn't know it. I was home alone—we were living together, sharing a condominium, but Reggie wasn't there when two hulks literally kicked in the door and came in."

The memory sent a chill through her.

"Yeah, I think that qualifies as terrifying," Gideon said, shock apparent on his handsome face. "Did they hurt you?"

"No, but there was…some physical contact and a distinct threat." Another chill went through her as she thought back to how one of the men had had her arms locked behind her back and the other had raised his fist to her…

"They got in my face," she said without going into detail. "They said they knew who I was, that I could afford to pay them. Reggie owed them ten thousand dollars—he'd been betting on basketball—"

"Don't tell me he'd used your name and his connection to you as collateral," Gideon said.

"I don't know. Maybe. Or they just assumed on their own that a connection with a Camden was enough to insure his debt. I just know they wanted the ten thousand dollars and they wanted it right then."

"That's bad…" Gideon said with a dark frown.

"I was scared. I was trying to figure out a way to actually get them the money just to save my own neck when my brother Cade and two of my cousins got there—they were bringing over a piece of furniture GiGi had given me and it was pure luck that they showed up right then. Apparently intimidating me was more fun than dealing with three other men because the thugs got out of there in a hurry and Cade and my cousins took me to GiGi's house."

"And they didn't tell you to get rid of the guy then and there?"

"No, actually I don't think they trusted themselves to say anything because they were all really, really quiet. They just got me out of there and sort of circled the wagons at GiGi's in case the hulks showed up there, too."

"Did you call the cops?"

"We called the police from GiGi's. But I didn't know who the men were—it wasn't as if they'd given me their business cards. I described them, and of course if they'd ever been found they could have been charged with breaking and entering. I gave the police Reggie's information so they could try to get him to tell them who they were, but I knew he wouldn't. I can't imagine what thugs like that might have done to him if he did."

"And then…"

"I ended it with Reggie. Believe me, two angry, giant, threatening men breaking your front door away from the frame and barging into your house will definitely scare you straight. I kept thinking what if I had had a baby or a couple of kids when that happened? Until then I thought it was only money that was at risk with Reggie, but after that? There was no way I would bring kids into that situation. I not only broke it off with Reggie, I told him not to come anywhere near me or my family again. He left town not long after that. I heard he'd moved to Las Vegas but I hope that isn't true because I can't imagine anywhere worse that he could go."

"And that was when you decided you weren't going to waste any more time on men," Gideon concluded, bringing the conversation full circle.

"It broke my heart to have to admit that Reggie and I couldn't have a future together. But the thought of how much more time it would take to start over from square one was almost as bad. I turned thirty this year—this month—and I'd let four more years go by. Years I couldn't afford to let go by. I knew I just didn't have the time to spare and if I really want a family—"

"And you *really* want a family—"

"I do. So I decided that I just have to have one."

He nodded his understanding. Then he said, "You know you're kind of messing with my head?"

"I am?" Jani said, perplexed.

Gideon laid an arm along the top of the sofa back and eased her hair slightly away from her face with his index finger. "To me the Camdens have always been the fat cats—bigger than life, above the problems the rest of us face, made of polished glass so trouble just rolls right off."

"I wish trouble just rolled right off," Jani interrupted. "But everybody has stuff. Stuff that sticks. It doesn't matter who you are."

"Yeah, and now you keep making me see that. You lost your parents when you were a little kid and got up-rooted from your home, your room, the kind of comfort zone a kid needs. You had to deal with maybe not being able to have the one thing you really want, a basic that everybody figures they can have—a family. You got involved with a guy who took advantage of you, who wasted time you don't have and put you in danger on top of it… You've had some hard knocks of your own. And then you go and rise above them—you aren't bitter, you come out all resilient and still positive and making the best of things… What's up with that?" he ended on a lighter tone.

"Sorry?" Jani apologized jokingly.

"I want to not like you, you know?" he said in a quiet voice. "But you just won't let me do that.…"

"I could spill red wine on your nice not-kid-friendly white carpet. Would that help?" she offered.

Gideon laughed, bringing a sparkle to those green eyes. "It's just a carpet. That probably wouldn't help."

"Well, let's see—after all, we can't have you liking a Camden…" Jani pretended to reach for her glass and Gideon caught her by the wrist. His hand was big and strong as he brought her arm back and kept hold of it on the cool leather between them.

"Yeah, you're not supposed to be cute and funny, either," he said.

There was a warmth in the way he was looking at her that made everything but the moment and the man drift away for Jani.

What was there about him, she wondered, knowing she wasn't supposed to be feeling so comfortable with him, knowing she wasn't supposed to be silently urging him to kiss her again the way he had in the parking lot that afternoon. Knowing she wasn't supposed to be thinking or feeling any of what she was thinking and feeling.

But when he went on looking into her eyes, when he pulled her forward by the wrist, when he leaned in to meet her halfway and did kiss her?

She couldn't find even an inkling of willpower to resist. She could only close her eyes and kiss him back.

He pulled her nearer then, his other hand going to the side of her face in a caress so tender she wanted to nuzzle into it and purr. But at the same time his lips were parting over hers and she was following her inclination to deepen the kiss instead, as it became more intimate than any they had shared in the past.

Wow, could the man kiss! There was a kind of pure, raw talent in those lips that Jani had never encountered before. Pure, raw talent and something primal and so sensual that it just made her melt into it.

He went on kissing her and somehow she found herself even nearer to him. Near enough to press her palm to his rock-hard chest, to let her other hand float up to his nape when he released her wrist and wrapped his arm around her.

There was something especially nice about the way he did that, too. The way he held her. All powerful and in control, yet gentle at the same time, making her feel swept into his arms even though no sweeping had occurred.

Their mouths opened wider and his tongue made an appearance at just the right moment, just when something more seemed called for.

Jani didn't balk; instead she reveled in his adeptness, enjoying the games he played that engaged and teased and toyed with her, tempting her into the mix with a sexy lure.

He hadn't offered to show her the bedrooms and Jani hadn't wondered about them. But she developed a sudden curiosity about the master suite. About the bed he slept in. About what it might be like to be taken to it...

But when it struck her that the thought was actually going through her mind, it rocked her a little. She couldn't be thinking about his bedroom. His bed. Being taken to it. What was she doing?

And that was when she recalled what she'd come into this evening telling herself. That she had had every intention of avoiding another kiss from Gideon, and that she'd had good reason for that.

Ground rules! she mentally shrieked at herself. *Dial it back and stick to those rules!*

Which would have been easier to do if she'd wanted to. But kissing him was so wickedly divine...

Still, she knew she couldn't let it go on. She certainly couldn't let it go even further, in the direction she'd been thinking about.

So she pushed slightly against his chest, trying hard not to note how much her fingers wanted to dig into it instead, and her tongue retreated at the same moment to compound the message.

Gideon got it.

The kiss grew chaste, and then ended. Only to be followed by another, as if he needed just one more morsel before he really could stop.

Then he inhaled deeply and sat back, shaking his head.

"We've come from really different places and we're headed down really different paths," he said in a deep, raspy voice that was so quiet she was almost not sure he was talking to her. "Why isn't that carrying the kind of weight it should be and keeping this on the straight and narrow?"

"I don't know..." Jani said, as quiet and as dumbfounded as he seemed to be.

"I like you and I'm not supposed to—that doesn't help," he said, half joking.

"Wine on the carpet?" she offered again.

He laughed. "I'm pretty sure you could throw it in my face and it wouldn't help."

"If that's what you want…" Jani teased, again pretending to reach for the glass.

And again Gideon caught her wrist.

And again Gideon kissed her—only lightly this time. But it was another kiss that Jani didn't want to end, in spite of everything.

Except that somehow her willpower had found a bit of a hold.

Apparently, so had his because this kiss was short-lived.

"I should get home," she said before he had the chance to start again. She didn't trust herself, either; that bit of willpower she'd mustered was already weakening.

Gideon conceded with a lift of his chin. He stood up and got her coat from the closet while Jani grabbed her purse and went to the door.

"I'll go down to the garage with you," he offered.

And then there would be more opportunities for kissing—in the elevator, at her car…

"No, no," Jani said. "There's an attendant and security cameras all over and I'm parked two spaces from the elevator. I'll be fine. Really!" she added for emphasis.

He brought her coat to her and held it for her to slip into, and she knew he was having as much difficulty keeping to the straight and narrow as she was when his hands went to her shoulders from behind for a moment while she fastened the buttons.

But then he let go, and she turned to face him with something she knew would put a damper on everything.

"Sunday dinner…" she said, doubting that he needed

any more of a reminder than that to know she was asking if he was coming.

"At your grandmother's house. To get the check to start the community center," he said, his tone distinctly more somber, making it clear he was not at all enthusiastic about the prospect.

"We're not ogres…"

"*That's* what I need—grow a big green head, would you?"

"By tomorrow? I can try, but I can't make any promises."

He was looking very intently at her and she knew he didn't want to agree to Sunday dinner. But she thought that she might be what was keeping him from a flat no, so she said, "Remember that you'll be my *special* guest."

He laughed at her outrageously naughty spin on what her grandmother had said, and she was glad he knew she was only kidding.

"Come on," Jani urged without any guile. "Just come. If you hate it you can whisper that in my ear, I'll get you the check and you can leave."

He didn't want to. She could see that.

But then he took another deep breath and said with all his reluctance in his tone, "Okay."

Jani had the answer she needed and thought she should go before he changed his mind, so she opened the door a crack as she said, "I'll text you my address. Come to my place at four and we'll go over together."

He nodded and Jani thought she'd sufficiently changed the tone of things to prevent any more kissing.

But no sooner had she thought that than he took both

of her arms in his massive hands and pulled her into another very sound good-night kiss.

Then he let her go and opened the door the rest of the way for her.

"Big green head. By tomorrow," he commanded as she went to the elevator.

"I'll do my best," she assured him as she pushed the elevator button and the door opened instantly.

She got in and turned to find Gideon standing in his doorway watching her, looking for all the world the way she felt—as if he would have done anything for this evening not to be ending.

But then the doors began to close and Jani called a last-minute, "Good night. And thanks for dinner!"

And she fought the urge the whole way down to the parking garage not to hit the button for his floor again and just go right back up and into his arms...

"Ground rules," she whispered to herself as the elevator came to a stop and the doors opened to the garage where a man was waiting to get on.

Only then did she notice that her finger was actually poised over the button for the seventh floor.

She yanked her hand back, took a deep breath and exhaled.

But she finally managed to get out of that elevator and go home.

Chapter Eight

"I don't know what's wrong with me, Jack," Gideon confided in his friend over breakfast the next morning at a small diner down the street from Gideon's loft.

His friend's response was a wry, humorless imitation of a laugh. "After yesterday's round of battles with Tiffany on the phone, hearing Sammy crying in the background because she was screaming at me, yeah, there's a side of me that doesn't know what's wrong with you, either. That side of me thinks there has to be something wrong with you *not* to run as fast as you can from *any* woman. Unfortunately, there's the other side of me."

"That saw Jani getting off the elevator in the garage last night when you were getting on," Gideon guessed.

Jack had shown up unexpectedly minutes after Jani had left. Gideon had been hoping the knock on his door meant she'd changed her mind and come back. Instead he'd opened it to his distraught friend. After it had become apparent that Gideon had hoped Jack was some-one else, Gideon had explained the situation and they figured out that Jack had just had his first glimpse of Jani downstairs.

From then on they'd talked about Jack's troubles. Then they'd scheduled this breakfast and Jack had left Gideon to get back to thinking about Jani. To wishing Jani *had* been outside his door instead of his friend. To reliving their kisses. And wanting to kiss her again. And to wanting to do more than kiss her...

Which was why this morning's breakfast conver-sation was about Gideon's demons rather than Jack's.

"Yeah, unfortunately there's that other side of me that saw January Camden last night," Jack confirmed. "And that woman is *something*. What did you call her? *A hot little number?* No truer words than those! Who wouldn't be blinded by that?"

It chafed at Gideon to hear his own early description of Jani repeated by his friend. It seemed disrespectful and demeaning. But what was he going to say to Jack? That his opinion, his feelings about Jani were different now? That would be admitting that there *were* feelings about Jani now. For Jani...

He didn't even want to *think* about that, let alone admit it.

"Blind is not a good thing," he said rather than ad-dressing any of the rest of it. "I can't lose sight—"

"Of her being a Camden, I know. But whoa! She's gorgeous! All that great hair and those eyes? Those are some of the most beautiful eyes I've ever seen!"

His friend's admiration prompted a wave of jealousy in Gideon on top of everything else...

"It's crazy," he muttered more to himself than to

Jack. Then to Jack, he said, "She's a damn Camden, and she wants kids in the worst way. Worse than any woman I've ever met. It's like fate is laughing in my face. Not only is she a member of a family that victimized mine, but she's also kid-obsessed. One or the other makes her poison to me and she's *both!*"

"So you want to be totally turned off by her," Jack said.

"But every time I'm with her, I forget all about her last name or who her relatives are. I even forget the baby stuff the minute she's not telling me about it."

"And *you* just want *her* in the worst way," Jack summarized, using Gideon's own words. "Forbidden fruit?" Jack suggested.

Gideon shrugged, unsure himself.

"So, just out of curiosity," Jack said cautiously, "if she *wasn't* a Camden, would you cave on the kid thing? Do you really mean it about no more kids in your life *ever?*"

"I really mean it," Gideon said without wavering. "You love a kid like you never knew you could love anything—you know that."

"I do," Jack agreed. "It's kind of a shock how much."

"And now you know what it's like to have them ripped away from you."

Jack didn't say anything to that. He didn't have to. The dark stare he was sending at his juice glass was confirmation enough.

"I'm not getting anywhere near another kid. *Ever!*" Gideon said.

"So you're right—January Camden is double trouble. But you want to be all over her, anyway."

This time it was Gideon who stared daggers at the

orange juice. "Which is why I don't know what's wrong with me."

Jack laughed another wry laugh, this one with a touch of humor to it. "There's nothing wrong with you. You're just a normal, healthy, red-blooded American boy with one of the most luscious pieces of—"

"Don't call her that!" He had to stop his friend before the word came out of Jack's mouth because he just couldn't let Jani be denigrated that way.

Jack merely said, "There's nothing wrong with you. There would be something wrong with you if you *weren't* tempted by a woman like that. I'm in the middle of divorce agony and cringing at the thought of another relationship, and I still couldn't take my eyes off her last night. I watched her walk all the way to her car before I pushed the elevator button to close the doors."

Gideon felt another wave of jealous resentment that he couldn't understand.

"Yeah, well, normal or not, it doesn't help," he groused. "And now I'm stuck going to dinner with the whole Camden clan tonight."

"That'll be weird," Jack commiserated. "Going to their house. Being with all of them. I'm surprised you agreed to it."

"Yeah, I'm not even sure how I did. You just don't expect to get steamrolled by a little old lady—I didn't see that coming and didn't have much time to mount a defense. Then last night with Jani—"

"Going to dinner at her grandmother's house means you'll see her and you were too hot for her to say no."

Gideon didn't bother to deny that. "Geez, I'm pathetic," he moaned disparagingly instead.

Jack laughed genuinely—but sympathetically—then.

"It's only one dinner and you'll come away with the start-up money for the community center. Let's think of it like that."

"Okay, let's think of it like that," Gideon concurred sarcastically.

"Then maybe you should try to find a way to get this woman out of your system," his friend suggested.

"Detox? Is there a rehab center to conquer addiction to a Camden?"

Jack shrugged elaborately. "Or sometimes you gotta dive in all the way before you can come out on the other end...."

Gideon didn't respond to that.

He was too worried that his friend might be right.

And that one way or another, he couldn't keep himself from diving in when it came to Jani.

He just had to hope he *did* come out on the other end.

And without the kind of scars and consequences the Camdens had left before...

Ordinarily Jani loved Sunday dinner at GiGi's. It was a big family gathering where everyone was free to bring as many guests as they wanted.

Seth, the oldest of the Camden grandchildren, lived in Northbridge, Montana, so he could only come when he was in town. But the remaining nine never missed a Sunday. And now that Cade was engaged, his fiancée, Nati Morrison, was also there every week to share the meal, along with her grandfather—and GiGi's companion—Jonah.

Tonight several of Jani's cousins had brought friends and Nati had also brought her friend Holly, so—along with Margaret and Louie who also always attended as extended family rather than household staff—it was a large group.

Such a large group that Jani was certain she alone was aware of how reserved Gideon was.

But he *was* extremely reserved.

When anyone approached him, he was amiable and friendly. When spoken to, he engaged in conversation and seemed interested. Jani had seen him talking sports and laughing with her brothers and cousins—who made great effort to get to know him and include him. He was polite and cordial to GiGi and had even stiffly accepted the hug the older woman insisted on giving him. And he'd had a lengthy talk with Jonah.

But now that Jani had experienced the relaxed Gideon, she knew the stiffer, more formal version when she saw it. And she saw it all through dinner, dessert and still now when she came from the kitchen with containers of leftovers that GiGi was sending home with her and with Gideon. Jani was reasonably sure that he hadn't spent even one minute of the evening relaxed or comfortable.

He was literally standing with his back to a wall as she went to him. And although he was in the living room with everyone else, he was about as near to the front door as he could get, as if he might slip out at any moment.

There was also such a tightness to his facial muscles that every line of his handsome face was more sharply etched.

Not that he didn't look fantastic, because he did. After texting to ask how to dress for the evening, he'd shown up in a dark gray sweater that zipped from midchest to the top of a mock neck. He'd left the zipper halfway down so he didn't appear stuffy; the open sides accentuated his jawline and made him look dashing and daring.

He had paired the sweater with low-rise charcoal pants that rode his hips and cupped his derriere so well Jani had caught more than one of the other women there stealing glances.

But regardless of how fantastic he looked, he also looked like someone who needed to be given a break and shepherded out of there before he made an escape on his own. So when Jani reached him she said, "We're all set. My grandmother just wants to say good-night to you and we can go."

Gideon only nodded, as if he didn't want to seem rude and show too much relief at the idea that he was minutes from the end.

Jani was glad when GiGi worked her way through the room at just that moment.

"I'll get our coats," Jani said, leaving Gideon to her grandmother, who had already given him the check for the community center without fanfare earlier in the evening so that their contribution would remain discreet.

The coat closet was nearby and she could hear the exchange of farewells between Gideon and her grandmother. She could hear that Gideon said all the right things—complimenting GiGi on the meal, and thanking her for dinner and for the check. Jani could also hear GiGi telling him how glad she was that he'd come and inviting him back anytime. When Jani returned, GiGi squeezed his upper arm rather than repeating the hug she'd first greeted him with, told Jani she'd talk to her tomorrow and left them to their coats.

Jani led the way into the entry where she set the leftover containers on the table beneath the crystal chandelier that hung down from the high ceiling. After accepting his coat from her, Gideon set it on the table, too, and took Jani's coat to hold for her.

Tonight Jani had on black slacks and a sweater Margaret had knitted her for Christmas. It was a bright red cable-knit with an off-the-shoulder scalloped neckline that folded over to drape down past her breasts. The drape provided a second layer of concealment making a bra unnecessary. So Jani hadn't worn one.

She slipped her arms into her black knee-length wool coat and Gideon lifted it onto her shoulders, brushing her bare skin as he did. Tiny tingles rained through her and she felt her nipples tighten instantly, but she worked to give no indication that such an innocent thing could do so much to her. She hoped she'd succeeded—the last thing she would want Gideon to know was that that was all it took to send her to the brink of being turned on. Instead she reached around with one hand to take her hair out of her collar and then grabbed the leftover containers from the table to hold in front of her like a shield.

"Okay, we can go!" she said glibly, still trying to conceal the effects of her brief contact with him. Effects that were compounded when she watched him shrug those broad shoulders into his leather jacket.

After that, the chill of the winter air when they stepped onto the landing outside the oversize front door was just what she needed.

Gideon had met her at her house but then insisted on driving. His car was parked pretty far back in the line of vehicles that surrounded the fountain at the center of the circular drive and even continued down the short private lane that led from Gaylord Street.

Neither of them said anything as they walked to it, and Jani only muttered a soft "Thanks" for Gideon opening the passenger door for her. He didn't respond before he closed the door and went around to get behind the wheel and start the engine.

"That wasn't too bad, was it?" Jani asked when they were settled.

"No," he said without conviction.

"It was awful? Horrible? You had a terrible time and the food made you sick?"

"No, none of that," he said with an involuntary laugh.

"This is just the way you are when you have a fabulous time?"

He kept his eyes on the road. "Your family couldn't have been nicer or more cordial—and it wasn't phony in any way. They made me feel like one of them. It looks like that's what they do with everybody. I was worried your grandmother might make some big production out of giving me the check, but she handled that great, too. She—all of your family—they're down-to-earth, regular people—"

"Because we aren't from Mars," Jani joked.

That got no response.

"The food was great," Gideon went on. "And there's even lunch for tomorrow. How can I complain about that? And that house…" He breathed an admiring sigh. "That's some house."

"So this *is* you after a fabulous time?"

He let silence fall for a moment before he said in a quiet, solemn voice, "I just kept looking around at the grandeur of that house, at all of your family, and picturing the dark, dreary bar and the small apartment above it that was the center of *my* family life. And what my family ended up like..."

Oh.

"You live in a really nice place now, too," she reminded him in a way she hoped was diplomatic.

"Yeah, but it didn't come at anyone else's expense," he said quietly. Then Jani saw him shrug. "It was just tough to separate things tonight. And not to feel guilty and disloyal for being where I was, for *not* having a miserable time or... You know, for *not* disliking you all..."

So he hadn't actually hated her family and having Sunday dinner with them. And he was beating himself up for it.

Jani understood that he was struggling with it all, but she wasn't quite sure what to say. She didn't know whether to apologize or not.

They'd reached her house again by then and when Gideon pulled into her driveway she decided maybe it was time to tell him her side of things, that maybe in some way it would help.

Besides, they might have been together for the past few hours, but there had been so many other people around that she didn't feel as if she'd spent any real time with him and she wasn't ready to have the evening end yet. Especially not with the way things stood now with Gideon.

"Come in for a while," she suggested.

"I probably shouldn't—"

"Come in, anyway. I don't know if it'll make any difference—maybe it will make things worse... I hope not, but let's finally talk about what happened in Lakeview."

He made a sound that wasn't quite a laugh. "Ah, the elusive other side of the story..."

"Come on…" Jani cajoled. "I already gave you the tour of my house when you first got here, but I can make coffee or tea or pour wine or whatever, and we can talk a little."

Gideon turned only his head to look at her, and Jani had the impression that if she were anyone else, there was no way he would agree to this.

But then he smiled a small, reluctant smile and said, "Okay."

Jani was so happy that he wasn't going to end the evening right then and there that she got out of the car before he'd even turned off the engine. She had her front door unlocked and open by the time he got there.

"What's your pleasure?" she asked once they were inside and taking off their coats.

Gideon's laugh this time was genuine and wicked before he said, "I had enough to eat and drink at your grandmother's."

"Okay, then let's just sit," Jani suggested, leading him into the living room to the left of the entry.

She flipped the switch that lit the lamps on the end tables bracketing the couch. Her house was decorated in a country-cottage style that made it warm and homey, and she was always glad to get back to it. Now she hoped Gideon had the same feeling.

He did seem more relaxed than he had at GiGi's, more the way he'd come to be with Jani as he sat on her buttery-soft overstuffed leather sofa.

Jani started a fire in the gas fireplace and then joined him. Kicking off her shoes, she sat sideways on the couch and tucked her feet under her so she could look directly at him.

Gideon was sitting with one arm outstretched across

the back of the sofa cushions and even though he was angled slightly in her direction, he still had one foot on the floor, the other ankle resting on his knee, keeping a little distance, Jani thought.

"Okay, let's have it," he said. "H. J. Camden's side of the story."

"H.J. and your great-grandfather really were friends, you know." Jani felt the need to remind him even though she had said it to him before. "They met not long after H.J. moved to Denver. They both belonged to some businessmen's association. H.J. considered Franklin his first friend in Colorado."

Jani could tell that Gideon was biting back a retort and she appreciated his restraint, knowing that had this been the first night they'd met he would be saying something along the lines of *with friends like that who needs enemies....*

"H.J. honestly went into the whole Lakeview deal with the intention of helping out Franklin," she said.

"He went into it with the intention of finding a cheap place to build factories and warehouses in close proximity to Denver," Gideon amended with some challenge in his tone.

"I'm not saying it wasn't to H.J.'s advantage, too. I'm saying that when it started, H.J. thought of it as one hand washing the other—Lakeview's location made it the best place for the factories and warehouses, but he needed rezoning to build there. Lakeview needed a new direction for its economy because it was dying as a farm community. As mayor, Franklin wanted to attract new business, housing, everything it took to turn it from a dying farm community to a prosperous suburb."

"Which was what H.J. promised in return for the

rezoning. Those were the promises that my great-grandfather made to his constituents and to the city council in order to *get* the rezoning."

"But the promises weren't empty," Jani insisted. "H.J. had a dozen stores by then but he decided that in order to expand to the extent he wanted to expand, to be able to offer the low prices that brought his customers into his stores, he needed to start manufacturing a lot of what he sold, and he needed to be able to warehouse what he could buy cheap if he bought in bulk."

"Which is why he wanted the factories and warehouses," Gideon supplied.

"Yes, but he also genuinely wanted Lakeview to benefit and for your great-grandfather to get the credit for being the forward-thinking mayor who was responsible for the progress that would save Lakeview. And it wasn't just talk—H.J. had a developer, a planner, a builder, a contractor lined up. He had blueprints and maps of the new Lakeview—a suburban area with affordable middle-class homes, schools, parks, shops and office buildings to bring in new businesses."

"None of which materialized."

"Because everyone H.J. had lined up turned on him," Jani said.

"The developer, the planner, the contractor, the builder all turned on H. J. Camden?" Gideon said in disbelief.

"They banded together and tried to extort a quarter of a million dollars from him. They said either he paid them that *bonus,* or they'd go somewhere else to build."

Gideon looked steadily at Jani and she could see the wheels of his mind working. Not necessarily in her favor.

Then he said with skepticism still echoing in his voice, "They all stood to make money by developing and building there. That's what they were in business to do. Why extort H. J. Camden on top of it?"

"Because even back then the Camden name brought out the greed in some people. I told you, there were a dozen stores by then, H.J. had made a name for himself."

"And a fortune."

"And a fortune—that's the point. Demanding the *bonus* was just a way they thought they could squeeze him and line their own pockets. They knew H.J. and Franklin were friends, and that Franklin had gone out on a limb making H.J.'s promises. It was pay up or else, and they were sure H.J. would pay up."

"And he wouldn't."

"Even doing well, in 1950s dollars, that would have bankrupted H.J. He had to hope that they were bluffing," Jani told Gideon, knowing that was what H.J. had written in his journal. "He thought there was enough opportunity for them in Lakeview and that even though he refused to pay them the bonus, they would still go through with everything."

"But they didn't."

"They didn't," Jani said somberly. "They went into North Denver and did everything there instead."

"And rather than paying the bonus that the people *he'd* lined up were holding out for, rather than going out and beating the bushes for a new set of people to fulfill his promises, since H. J. Camden had what he wanted, he just let my great-grandfather take the fall."

"He did try to find new people," Jani said. "But everything that was supposed to be done in Lakeview was being done in North Denver, and other builders, contractors and developers were convinced that people would go to North Denver rather than to Lakeview—"

"Because by then what Lakeview did have were factories and warehouses that people *didn't* want to live near. Because H. J. Camden had gotten what *he* wanted," Gideon repeated.

Jani couldn't deny that because it was true and she wanted to be honest with him. "Yes," she admitted. "But H.J. regretted that Franklin took the blame. He did go to Franklin and try to persuade him to come to work for Camden Incorporated himself. In an executive position. He offered to get your great-grandfather out of Lakeview, away from it all. But Franklin turned him down."

"Because then it would have really looked like my great-grandfather had just been in league with H.J. to mislead the community that had elected and trusted him. Because he felt a loyalty to Lakeview, an obligation to stay and still try to redevelop, to do some of what H.J. had promised."

"But if H.J. couldn't do it…"

"Yeah, certainly my great-grandfather couldn't. Especially when he was under attack by the same people he was trying to help. People who didn't trust him anymore. Who believed that everything he said was a lie. Who wanted him to pay for what happened. It took the next mayor to even bring in cheap housing for the factory and warehouse workers, and what went along with building *that* community instead."

"So why didn't Franklin cut and run?" Jani asked. "Why did he wait to have his house burned to the ground and basically get chased out of town? Why didn't he go to work for H.J.? Or even go to H.J. after all that happened?"

"He wasn't too sure that H. J. Camden *hadn't* just used him. And even if he gave H.J. the benefit of the doubt, he thought that to go to work for Camden Incorporated—in an executive position—would prove the worst of the accusations against him. He didn't want that. Even while he was sweeping floors in that damn bar he still held out hope that eventually he might find a way to clear his name—although I don't know how he thought he was going to do that. Mostly, he just wasn't the kind of person who could live with himself if he came out on top while the people who had trusted him lost out."

"So he sacrificed and punished himself instead. And the rest of his family to come."

"Don't put any of this on my great-grandfather," Gideon said sternly. "It crushed him that he'd disappointed people who had relied on him. That a whole community that he'd been responsible for had been hijacked and screwed over because of him. That he couldn't come through for them in the end. It broke him."

"I'm sorry," Jani said sincerely. "But isn't there some part of you that can see H.J.'s side, too? You're a businessman—what if people you had on board for something tried to force you to pay them for more than the job they were going to do because they thought they had you over a barrel? Yes, H.J. could have built one less factory or one less warehouse and paid the bonus, but you know—I know and H.J. knew—that if he caved to extortion once, it was only a matter of time before they would do it again. And again…"

Gideon shook his head. "No, I wouldn't have paid extortion money. But I would have—I *would*—do anything I had to do to make good on my word."

Jani believed that. And that for a man like him it was difficult to forgive H.J. for having done so much less.

"The bottom line," Gideon said, "is that when it came to a choice between H. J. Camden's own interests and the interests of Lakeview and my great-grandfather—"

"H.J. went with his own interests," Jani conceded because she knew H.J. couldn't be completely vindicated. "I'm not condoning the choices he made. I'm not condoning the fact that he didn't do anything at all for Lakeview when the deal he had in place fell through. I just want you to see that there *was* another side. That going in, H.J. had good intentions and wasn't just using Franklin and his position as mayor. H.J. truly meant for it to work out, and for the whole thing to be a huge feather in Franklin's political cap. He actually thought that it might put Franklin in a position to run for governor…"

"Yeah, I know that part," Gideon admitted. "My great-grandfather thought that together he and H. J. Camden were going to do big things for the entire state. He just said the joke turned out to be on him."

"I'm sorry." Jani covered Gideon's hand where it rested on the back of the couch and squeezed it to let him know how genuinely she meant that.

Gideon spent a moment in brooding silence, staring at his leg propped atop his other knee, before he turned his hand to take hers and looked into her eyes.

He inhaled deeply and then exhaled as if he actually might be letting go of some of the resentments that had been stirred tonight.

Then he said, "You didn't have anything to do with it."

"Or you…" she pointed out. "And now you *are* doing good for Lakeview—redeveloping it, making improvements…"

"And hopefully the article will clear the name of Franklin Thatcher so it really can be honored with the community center."

"I just wanted you to know that it wasn't all an evil plot from the beginning. That H.J. didn't do anything maliciously. He meant well, even if he didn't come through in the end. So maybe you don't need to see us all now as descendants of the devil…"

"If only my great-grandfather had had less integrity, less conscience, our families might be old friends today?" he joked wryly.

Jani was happy that he was trying for a lighter tone. She shrugged helplessly. "I don't know what to say to that… Yes, that would probably have been the case. But no matter what, I—we all—just want to make up for what happened in whatever way we can now."

After another moment of merely staring at her, into her eyes, Gideon increased his grip on her hand and said, "It's okay. I didn't know about the extortion plot before this, and yes, I can see some of where H.J. was coming from. It doesn't change what my family went through after the fact, but I guess it is good to know that H.J. didn't just use my great-grandfather."

"H.J. honestly liked and respected him," Jani said. "He was sorry to lose his friendship." Which was something else that H.J. had written in his journal.

"So he'd be glad to have me sitting here with his great-granddaughter, holding her hand?" Gideon asked with the elevation of just one eyebrow and a bad-boy glimmer to the smile he gave her.

"Well now, *that* I can't say—Lindie, Livi and I were all fourteen when he died so we weren't dating yet, but we *were* teenagers and boys had started to notice us all, and there wasn't *anything* that H.J. liked about *that!* He actually caught me kissing one of my cousin's friends in the backyard—my first kiss when I was thirteen—and H.J. went after him with a rake."

"Must have been a hot kiss…"

"Hardly. It was my first—remember? It was awkward and pinch-lipped and the guy still got chased by a crazy old man with a rake."

"So I guess I have two things to be grateful for…" Gideon said with an amused smile.

"Two things?" Jani parroted.

The strain that had surrounded their conversation about Lakeview seemed to have resolved itself and Gideon used his hold on her hand to pull her toward him as he repositioned himself so that he was facing her.

"That H. J. Camden is nowhere around with a rake, and that somewhere along the way you managed to get in some kissing practice—because you're not bad at it now…"

"Not bad?" She pretended to be insulted even though it was clear he was merely teasing her.

"Maybe you need just a little more practice…" he said before he leaned forward, and kissed her.

The strain had definitely been resolved because from the start there was no anger or resentment in that kiss, no aggression. It was calm and tranquil and somehow soothing, as if they were back on familiar and far more desirable terrain.

Gideon's lips parted, engaging her right from the start, inviting her in, and Jani breathed an involuntary sigh of relief as she let her lips part and kissed him in return. She knew she shouldn't be so happy to be back in this predicament, that she should count dinner, getting the check to him, and having told H.J.'s side of the story as accomplishment enough for one night, that she should be saying good-night to him and sending him home.

But she liked kissing him so much.

And when his free hand sluiced under her hair to cradle her head, she just raised her own hand to his chest and surrendered. Their mouths opened wider and his tongue began to circle hers as they picked up where they'd left off the previous evening.

Thoughts of anything else drained away then; what took over was something basic and fundamental and purely sensual. She melted toward him, into that kiss, and met his tongue with her own to answer his every tease and temptation, relinquishing herself to being with this man to whom everything in her was drawn.

She massaged and caressed his chest despite the barrier of his sweater, and she reveled in how hard and strong the muscles of his pectorals lurking just beneath it were. Hard and honed—feeling them made her want badly to see them, except that that would have meant breaking their kiss and she wasn't about to give that up.

He released her other hand and wrapped his arm around her to pull her up against him. Her own arm went naturally around him, closing even more of the distance between them and leaving only the breadth of her hand still resting on his chest to separate them.

Jani became very aware of how taut her nipples had

become behind the double shield of her sweater and its folded-over collar. Taut and so, so sensitive hiding there but striving for more.

She slipped her hand from his chest to his back, freeing the way for him to pull her completely up against him as if he knew how much she wanted that.

Her nipples grew harder still, diamond nubs insistently pressing into him as the kiss turned hungry and primal. But there was so much of his sweater and hers between them that it was an agony of obstruction.

Answering the need for even more closeness, Jani arched her spine, pressing her breasts firmly into the expanse of that powerful chest.

It didn't help ease much of her need but what did bring her hope was when Gideon found the hem of her sweater and slipped his hand under it to her bare back.

She could feel his long fingers, big and warm and strong, splayed out in the very spot where a bra would have fastened had she been wearing one.

She had the fleeting thought that when he realized she wasn't she might think she'd planned this, but she couldn't really care as he caressed her naked flesh and made her yearn for the feel of his hands on breasts that were crying for attention.

Their tongues continued to play a game that intensified as the desires rose in Jani. Gideon massaged her back, his head traveling in a slow path to the left of her spine, then to her side, then to the beginning swell of one breast.

He paused there as if waiting to be warned not to go any further, but that was the last thing on Jani's mind. Instead she gave the go-ahead with a deep breath that expanded her lungs and her chest in invitation for him to finish that trip.

And finish it he did—bringing his hand all the way over her breast and letting her oh-so-tight nipple nestle in his palm.

Never had she been so glad to be braless. And never had anything felt as good. His hand was the perfect fit; Jani's breast was like molding clay in his expert grip, yielding to his every touch, his every stroke, to the pure artistry he worked there. As he tugged and tickled and sweetly, sweetly tortured her, Jani felt any wisdom, any will to resist or put limits on him drifting away.

And yet even as she began to think of having his mouth where his hand was, of having his hand travel farther still, of making even better use of that long soft sofa, another thought managed to sneak in.

No matter how sublime the moment was—and it *was* sublime—it was only a moment. A moment right now. It wasn't what she was really about with Gideon. It wasn't why they were together, and there was no chance that it could lead to more.

And if it couldn't lead to more, then it couldn't be anything at all. Not even for a moment.

Much as she wished otherwise, she came half-heartedly to the realization that this couldn't go on. With a moan of regret, she resisted the urge to let her hands finish the course they'd set to get underneath his sweater and instead placed them both on his chest to push against him.

"We can't…" she managed to whisper, coming away from the heat of that kiss and dropping her forehead to the spot where his neck turned into his shoulder.

Gideon didn't say anything but she could feel the

fast pounding of his heart beneath her palm that told her stopping this wasn't any easier for him than it was for her.

But in spite of that, he turned his face to hers, kissed her temple gently, and with one parting pulse of his fingers into the soft flesh of her breast, he let go of her and took his hand away.

For a brief while they sat like that, in silence, Gideon's arms wrapped around her, holding her.

Then Jani heard him sigh a soft sigh before saying in a raspy-sounding voice, "I better go."

Because to stay would make it impossible to practice restraint and not to do more than they already had...

He didn't say it but Jani knew without a doubt that was what he was thinking.

It was what she was thinking.

She only nodded against him, still caught up in wanting to kiss him again, wanting to have his hand back on her naked breasts. In not wanting to lose those arms around her...

"It's just too good when it's only you and me..." he confided in a whisper, almost as if he were sorry it was true.

He kissed her temple again and Jani forced herself to sit up straighter, to veer back from him enough for him to stand.

She was slightly late in following suit because she wasn't too sure her legs were strong enough to hold her. But by the time he was shrugging into his coat she had joined him in the entry, her hands stuffed into the pockets of her pants, her elbows locked, her shoulders tensed nearly to her jawline to keep herself from reaching for him.

In a more businesslike voice that still bore the huskiness of desire, he said, "This week, blueprints and plans should be in a final form for you to see, if you—"

"Okay," Jani said too eagerly, glad for the chance to see him again because her mind was spinning out of control with wanting him and she couldn't think of any excuse herself.

"I'll be in touch..." he said.

Oh, how she hated the lack of certainty or real plans implied by that phrase!

But she only nodded again because what else was she going to do, ask to hire on as his personal assistant so they could spend every day together?

"I'll call you," he said.

Another ambiguous phrase that she'd never hated quite as much as she did right then. Right then, when she didn't want him to leave at all, when—if he did have to go—it would be so much easier if she knew exactly when they'd be together again.

But that wasn't how it was going to be and there was nothing she could do about it.

Gideon reached out and clasped one hand around the top of her right arm, squeezing tight and pulling her forward just slightly, enough for him to lean in and kiss her again with barely parted lips and a world of heat simmering behind them that she wanted so badly to tap into.

Then he did a second squeeze of her arm, released it, and let himself out her front door while she stayed standing in the middle of the entryway.

Wanting desperately for him to be in touch all right— in touch with every square inch of her....

Chapter Nine

"Still looking?"

"I am," Jani answered the nurse who had poked her head into the small room.

"Not to rush you but just to let you know, we close up at five. We'll probably have patients until a little after that tonight and you're welcome to stay until we're finished with them, but it won't be too much later. And you know this is your first run through of the donor book. You can take some notes and think about it for a while. You don't have to make a final decision right now."

"Okay, thanks," Jani said with a forced smile.

The nurse closed the door and Jani deflated a little.

She'd been at the reproductive endocrinologist's office since leaving work at two o'clock. It was four-thirty. And yes, she was having some trouble deciding on a donor, which she'd hoped to accomplish today. As soon as she picked one she could start the artificial insemination process.

But she was no closer to making her choice now than when she'd started. And she'd already been through the loose-leaf pages of the three-ring binder twice.

In fact, she didn't have even one Maybe.

It had taken her until the last profile on the first run-through to realize why that was.

If the donor didn't have green eyes, she didn't read any further.

If he wasn't at least six feet tall with an athlete's build, she didn't read any further.

If he didn't have sandy, golden-brown hair, she didn't read any further.

If there was a photograph included in the profile—which was the case for some of them—that was all it took for her to turn the page.

Because none of the men pictured looked anything like Gideon. In one way or another, this lack of resemblance was what had caused her to eliminate the rest on her initial search, too.

When that had occurred to her, she'd wondered if she'd lost her mind.

A brief time ago she hadn't even known this man. He certainly wasn't a candidate to father her baby now that she did. And the last thing she should be doing was counting out real possibilities because they didn't measure up to him in some way.

There was no reason whatsoever that Gideon should have any kind of an influence on this process.

After reminding herself of that she'd started at the beginning of the donor notebook a second time, determined that nothing about Gideon would be included in her criteria.

But her determination hadn't been enough; she'd

reached the end of the book a second time without a single possibility.

It was so ridiculous! she told herself.

She didn't have any illusions—despite the chemistry between them, Gideon still had a problem with her being a Camden. And while she might not know what was behind it, she did know that he was devoutly against having kids.

No Camdens.

No kids.

That was Gideon Thatcher's point of view in a nutshell.

And there was no changing another person's thinking, another person's long-held habits or desires or beliefs. There was no changing what was at someone's core.

Wanting them to be different didn't make them different. She'd learned that with Reggie.

And while she might think it was a shame that someone as good with kids as Gideon was should be adamantly against having any for some reason, she couldn't force him to any more than she could force Reggie to stop gambling.

So why were thoughts of Gideon interfering with her mission at the doctor's office today?

It shouldn't have come as a surprise.

Thoughts of Gideon had interfered with everything else this week.

It was Wednesday and she hadn't heard from him since he'd left her house on Sunday night. But there hadn't been a minute since then that he hadn't been on her mind. There hadn't been a single phone call she hadn't hoped was from him. There hadn't been a single outfit picked without the idea that he might somehow see her in it. There hadn't been a single night when he wasn't the only thing she could think about as she lay in her bed, a single night when she hadn't relived his kisses, closed her eyes and tried to feel his touch, when she hadn't wanted him so badly she'd ached.

But where was that going to get her? she asked herself, sitting in that windowless room.

It wasn't going to get her a baby.

And a baby was what she wanted.

In the same way that Reggie's need to gamble and Gideon's resentment of the Camdens weren't going to change, wanting a family wasn't going to change for her. It was what she'd always wanted. It was something she was willing to go to any ends to have. It was something she couldn't be happy or fulfilled without.

Which meant that she couldn't let anything or anyone put it off any longer.

Staring at the donor profile notebook, she was angry with herself for having let that happen today. She hadn't succeeded in choosing a donor this afternoon, and that was her own fault.

But she vowed that she wasn't going to let it happen again.

She couldn't hurry through making such an important choice now, at the end of the day, when she finally had her head straightened out. So she *had* lost today and however many more days it would take before she could get back here and set the wheels in motion. But she would come in again as soon as she could and read the profiles with a fresh eye and a clear head. Without Gideon being a factor in any way.

Because he wasn't.

He was just a really—*really*—good-looking guy whom she couldn't help liking and being attracted to regardless of all the obstacles. The insurmountable obstacles.

Whatever was happening with Gideon was just a little glitch that she had to get over.

And she would.

She'd get over that more easily than she would ever get over not having a family.

She wanted a baby, and she was going to have a baby before her time ran out.

And she wasn't going to let anything or anyone else put that in any more jeopardy than she already had.

The next time she went through that donor notebook she'd look for someone with *her* eye color, *her* hair color, *her* attributes.

Because it was going to be *her* baby!

But somehow when she got up from the table, intent on arranging another time to look through the profiles, Jani also knew that meeting Gideon had cast a shadow over this.

And all she could do was hope that at some point she'd be able to escape that shadow.

After leaving the doctor's office, Jani stopped in to see her grandmother. She wanted to discuss her idea for an additional way to compensate Gideon for what H.J. had done long ago—offer the Thatcher Group the opportunity to build all future Camden Superstores.

"From what I understand, the Thatcher Group is more about city planning than building one building at a time, but maybe our stores are large enough projects that Gideon would consider the offer. It would be another way to make things up to him. I know you want us to make as many amends as we can, and I can't think of anything beyond that—his life seems to be exactly the way he wants it, his business is successful, he has a beautiful place to live. He's the one member of the Thatcher family who pulled himself out of the ashes H.J. left and there isn't anyone else to make amends to. Plus, I don't think he wants to have that much to do with us—he accepted the community center for Franklin Thatcher's sake and for the sake of Lakeview, but when it comes to himself, I can't see him wanting a long relationship with us," she'd concluded, reminding herself at the same time that that was something she needed to keep in mind.

But GiGi wanted to at least provide an opportunity for more so she told her to make the offer of future building projects. If Gideon declined they would count the community center as his compensation, and move on to the next project.

Jani turned down her grandmother's invitation to dinner and left, feeling even more dejected at the idea that her excuses for seeing Gideon were dwindling.

At home she changed out of her work clothes into a pair of soft pink flannel pajama pants and a cuddly, tight white T-shirt with long sleeves and a scoop neck.

She'd just brushed out her hair, intending to put it into a ponytail, when her doorbell rang.

She wasn't expecting anyone. Gideon instantly came to mind the way he had been since he'd left here on Sunday night, so she let her hair fall free around her shoulders, called herself an idiot and ran for the front door.

Even with her hopes high, she'd still learned a harsh

lesson with Reggie, so she peered through her peephole the minute she reached her door.

And for the first time in three days her hopes weren't for naught—it was Gideon standing in the glow of her porch light.

Her heart pounded and her spirits skyrocketed even as she told herself to keep her perspective.

But she raced through unlocking all her locks, then opened the door with a grin she just couldn't suppress.

"Hi," she said, conveying her surprise in that single word.

"You can tell me to go away and not bother you if you want," he greeted in return. "But I have pizza."

"Pizza that smells really good," Jani countered as if it was the food she was happy to see. "I was just wondering what I was going to have for dinner."

"I've always been known for my impeccable timing," he joked with a ludicrously suggestive wiggle of one eyebrow.

Jani laughed, stepped back from the doorway and said, "Come in. But as you can see, I'm not dressed for entertaining." She was, however, glad that the T-shirt had a sort of built-in bra in the form of a second layer of fabric across the bust, because she wasn't wearing one.

"I'm not dressed for company, either. I worked alone from home today, got a little cabin fever and decided I could use some air so I ordered a pizza for pick-up. Then I hated the thought of going back home to eat it alone and since I wanted to say thanks, I thought I'd see if I could do it with a pie. It's from Kaos over on South Pearl. Have you had it?"

"I love Kaos!" she said, laughing at how that sounded as she closed the door behind him.

Kaos was an eclectic little place that made delectable thin-crust pizza.

"Fresh tomato sauce, mozzarella that I guess they make there, and everything else that sounded good," he said, raising the box. "You can take off anything you don't like."

"I like everything," Jani assured him, thinking that what she liked most was him and that it felt much, much too right to be with him again. "I also have a bottle of wine I can contribute—" That she'd bought as her last hurrah, to enjoy before she got pregnant.

"Why don't you take the pizza to the coffee table while I get the wine, and we'll really do this casual," she suggested.

In the kitchen, she quickly opened the wine and gathered glasses and napkins, and was back just as Gideon was taking off his leather jacket.

He was right—he wasn't dressed up. He was wearing a pair of old jeans that were threadbare in spots and a V-neck sweater with a white crewneck T-shirt showing underneath it.

Jani was glad that she wasn't the only one in lie-around-the-house clothes but it didn't change the fact that he looked terrific. And apparently he'd shaved in order to pick up his pizza. He also smelled of a woodsy cologne that made her want to just close her eyes and breathe him in.

But she resisted the urge.

They each sat down on the floor at opposite ends of her oval coffee table, with the pizza box in the center. Then Gideon opened the lid and Jani surveyed the fully loaded pie.

"Yum! I'm starving!"

They each chose slices from their respective sides and bit off the points, judging the pizza fantastic when they'd savored their bites. A little discussion about the wine followed before they settled into just enjoying the meal.

That was when Gideon said, "The *Lakeview Monthly* reporter emailed me his article. Apparently he talked to you yesterday?"

"He did," Jani said.

"I read what he wrote and wanted to say thanks. You, uh… You really cleared my great-grandfather's name."

"I just told the truth," Jani said between bites.

"More of it than I expected—"

She hadn't indicted H.J. in any way. Instead, she'd explained that the reason the original redevelopment of Lakeview had fallen through had nothing whatsoever to do with Franklin Thatcher. That it had been a result of an altercation between H.J. and the people H.J. had lined up to do the work.

"You said something about Franklin falling under the wheels of Camden progress," Gideon continued. "I didn't think I wanted him to look like a victim but—"

"He was," Jani said. "He was a victim who unfairly got the blame."

"Which you are also quoted saying in the article." Gideon paused a moment to drink his wine and seemed to consider his next words. "I don't know if this is crazy or weird or what, but I read the things you said, the way you said them, and it so openly set the record straight that it felt like a huge weight had been lifted off my shoulders."

Jani didn't take the bite of pizza crust she was about

to take and instead stared at him. "It was such a small thing…"

"I can't explain it. It was just that seeing it in writing, knowing it will be out there—in print, on the internet, *everywhere*… I don't know. I just think that anyone left who ever associated the name Franklin Thatcher with lies and deceit, really will know now that it's unfounded. It's like my great-grandfather finally received his pardon from the governor. And it was a relief to me that I hadn't expected."

Gideon raised his wineglass to her in mock toast. "So I wanted to say thanks."

"None necessary," Jani said quietly. All the Camden grandchildren agreed with GiGi that some sort of restitution should be made to the people H.J. had wronged, but until that moment Jani hadn't realized just how important this mission was. Or how gratifying it might be.

But her own gratification wasn't the point and she thought it better to accept Gideon's thanks without making a big deal out of it. So she went back to talking about how much she liked the food even though she couldn't eat any more.

Gideon said he'd had his fill, too, and after allotting Jani the leftovers and disposing of the box for her while she wrapped the last two slices, they refilled their wineglasses and returned to the living room, sitting on the sofa rather than the floor this time.

They both sat close to the center of the couch, facing each other.

"The pizza was a treat. I hate to order it for myself when I'm alone so I almost never do," Jani said.

"The downfall of the single life," Gideon said melodramatically.

"Is that the only one for you?" Jani asked, joking in return but also hoping she might get him to open up a little more about that part of himself. "Did divorce leave you a confirmed bachelor?"

"No," he answered without hesitation. "I'd like to get married again."

"Really," Jani said.

Gideon laughed. "Why does that shock you?"

She shrugged. "I just thought... I don't know, you seem so against having kids, I assumed the two go together."

"But they don't *have* to—aren't your plans proof of that?"

"Sure," she said. But he was making her all the more curious. "You liked being married but you didn't like having kids?"

His laugh was more melancholy this time. "I liked them both."

"Then you're just confusing me... You liked being married and having kids, you want to remarry, but there's absolutely no way you're ever having kids again?"

"That pretty much sums it up."

"I need to know the story that goes with this," she said bluntly. Then she regretted her words because she recalled wondering before if he'd lost a child tragically. She was afraid she'd been insensitive, so she added in a hurry, "If it's something you can talk about..."

But Gideon took a turn at shrugging. "There's no reason I can't talk about it. It just... You know how it is—divorce is not the highlight of my life."

"Is it worse than having creeps barge into your home and threaten you?"

He stretched an arm along the sofa back and used the knuckle of his index finger to brush her cheekbone consolingly. Then he said, "There was somebody I consider a lowlife involved but there weren't threats of bodily harm, no."

"So tell me," Jani urged.

He hesitated but then took a drink of his wine and said, "I reconnected with my high school sweetheart at our ten-year class reunion and she was fresh out of a rocky on-again-off-again marriage to a jerk."

"A lowlife jerk," Jani qualified.

Gideon laughed. "Definitely a lowlife jerk. Whom she'd divorced the week before the reunion. I figured it was really over and there wasn't any reason we couldn't pick up where we'd left off when we'd first gone our separate ways to college."

"You'd been serious before?"

"Yeah, reasonably. But not enough to trade a college education for marriage at eighteen—there was no way I was risking ending up like my father and my grandfather, in that damn bar... Anyway, Shelly had gone out of state to college and we'd kept in touch for a while, but you know how those things go, eventually it just fizzled and—"

"Ten years later you met up again."

"And things moved fast—that happens when you already knew each other and cared for each other and didn't have any kind of ugly breakup. Things moved so fast that by the time she realized she was pregnant with Trent's baby, she and I were engaged."

"Oh," Jani said.

"Yeah. Nothing's ever easy, is it?" he asked wryly. "But her ex was a lying, cheating jerk who had left her high and dry for other women three times, and fooled around on her in between those splits, so when she said she was through with him, that not even a baby could make her go back to him, I believed her." Another shrug. "And I was willing to be a father to her baby—"

"You were?"

"I was. I loved Shelly, and the baby seemed… I don't know, we'd already been together a month when she realized she hadn't just missed cycles out of stress—what she'd thought after an earlier home pregnancy test had been negative. Instead she found out late that she actually was pregnant. It wasn't such a stretch to think about the baby as sort of my own, so I just thought, okay, let's do this…"

Jani suffered a pang of regret that she hadn't met him when his thinking had been along those lines. But she ignored it.

"And the birth father?"

"When she told him she was pregnant—and showed him the doctor's report to prove through the timing that it was his—he said he didn't want anything to do with it, that the kid was her problem. Shelly swore that didn't bother her. She even seemed a little relieved that she wouldn't have to deal with the jerk about visitation or custody or anything, and I thought the whole thing was over and done with. So we got married," Gideon continued. "Shelly was five months pregnant at our wedding, and she and the baby were just going to be mine."

"Simple as that."

"That's how it seemed. And four months later we had a baby girl—Jillie—and it was all good.…"

Something about the way he said that made it hard for Jani to believe. "Only it wasn't?"

"No, it really was. I told you, I liked being married, having a kid." But he turned his head away as if he were seeing into the past, and the expression on his oh-so-handsome face wasn't joyful—he was frowning.

Then his green eyes came back to her and he said, "I never thought of myself as a kid person. I'm a guy—kids, babies, so what? I thought that someday I'd have some, but…I don't know…I just didn't really have a concept of what it was to be a parent."

"A lot of work…"

"Sure. But that didn't bother me. What I didn't realize was how you *feel* about a kid.…" He shook his head and returned to staring at the coffee table as if a part of him was reliving what he was talking about.

"I loved that kid like I didn't think it was possible to love anyone," he confessed. "She'd go to bed with sniffles, I'd get up in the middle of the night to make sure she wasn't sick. I'd hear on the news about something bad happening to a child, and I'd have to double-check our locks. All the plans for the future were with Jillie in mind, what would be best for her. I opened a college fund for her when she was six months old. We only took vacations to places where Jillie could come, too, so we didn't have to leave her behind. I'd take her to the park and watch her like a hawk."

"Sounds like being a parent."

"But it wasn't anything like what I thought. I lived and breathed for that kid…"

Jani could see that he'd tapped into amazing emotions as a parent, and again she had the fear that something awful had happened to the child.

But then he said, "Jillie was three when Shelly's ex popped up again. He said he changed his mind. He claimed he hadn't been able to shake knowing that he had a kid out in the world. He swore up and down that he'd be faithful if only Shelly would give him another chance because he wanted both Shelly and Jillie after all."

"Three years later?" Jani said incredulously.

"Yeah, it seemed too ridiculous to matter to me, too."

"But it *wasn't* ridiculous?"

The frown that creased his brow was almost answer enough. "She went back to him," he said flatly. "She *said* that she felt obligated, that Jillie should be raised by her *real* father. That they were the *real* family. But I think the truth was that the guy was like a drug to her. It was like drinking had been to my father. Or like your ex's gambling—"

"Demons," Jani said, referring to a comment Gideon had made when she'd told him about Reggie—that there was no fighting other people's demons.

"Shelly apologized and cried—there was genuine guilt there, I think. She said she honestly had thought he was out of her system. She thought she could be done with him, but—"

"She couldn't help herself," Jani finished for Gideon with the words she'd heard Reggie say too often.

"And when she left, she took Jillie."

And that was where his real pain had come from— Jani could see it, she could hear it in his voice.

"I wasn't the biological father, so I had no rights. It didn't make any difference that I'd been there when Jillie was born, that I'd fed her and changed her diapers, helped teach her to roll over and sit up and eat with a spoon. It didn't make any difference that I'd read to her every single damn night before bed—"

"The bear book…" Jani said.

"It didn't make any difference that Jillie was ninety-nine percent mine. Because of that one percent that made her biologically *not* mine, I was out and Trent was back in. Just that easy, and without my having a leg to stand on to fight it. Shelly and Trent decided to move to Arkansas where Trent was from, and I haven't seen Jillie since."

So that explained how he didn't have any kids even though he had had one.

"That was it for me," he went on, the strain coming through in spite of the lighter tone he was trying to take. "I loved Shelly. Wholeheartedly. But it wasn't the same as what I felt for Jillie. You love a kid unconditionally. It digs the kind of roots in you that you never knew anything could—"

"And you don't ever want that again?" Jani said in disbelief, thinking that having loved one child so much, he would want another.

"When a marriage ends—it's tough. It hurts. But you can talk yourself through it. But losing a kid you love? A kid who's nothing but pure joy to you? That's… There's no consolation."

"But you've sworn never to have any kids—a child who's biologically yours—"

He shook his head adamantly. "There aren't any *buts* for me. I've seen friends separated from their kids, reduced to being half-time parents or long-distance parents—my best friend is having to adjust to that particular form of hell right now—and if you think he's feeling any less than I felt, you're wrong. On whatever level, it's still losing your kid. And I won't ever risk going through that again. No kids, no chance for that kind of heartache. So, yeah, I'd get married again. But there won't ever be kids for me."

And once more it was glaringly evident that they were on different tracks in life.

But somehow, at that moment, that just wasn't how it felt to Jani. Especially when he smoothed her hair over her shoulder with his palm and smiled a lazy sort of smile at her.

"There you have it. And you're probably thinking that at least that tale of woe in my life isn't H. J. Camden's fault," he joked.

He really was making an effort to lighten the tone and Jani thought it better to go with that, so she half joked in return. "Actually it's because of him—in a roundabout way—that you were determined to get your education. Maybe he should get a little credit."

Gideon's response was very different from what it would have been when they'd first met. Now he laughed. "I'll give you that one because you pulled my great-grandfather out of the fire in that article."

"And because it's true," she challenged.

"Okay, yeah, in a roundabout—and not very admirable—way, H. J. Camden can have some credit for my getting an education."

"I'll take it even with the qualification," Jani decreed.

The tension from discussing his divorce seemed to be dissolving and for a moment neither of them said anything, letting go of it.

It occurred to Jani then to refill their empty wineglasses. It was just too nice to be sitting there with him—despite what they'd been talking about—and she didn't want to break the spell.

But just as she lifted the bottle, Gideon said, "I

should probably go and let you get back to whatever you had planned tonight."

Talk about a spell-breaker!

"Or we could have another glass of wine…" Jani suggested.

"We could…" he said as if that didn't interest him at all.

What did seem to hold his attention, though, was gazing into her eyes. And brushing featherlight strokes along the side of her face with his index finger, lulling her too much for her to move…

He took a deep breath and sighed. "I came here tonight to say thanks for the article but…I really sort of needed to see you."

"Is there a problem with the community center?"

"Nah. The problem is with me… I just couldn't go any longer… Sunday night feels like years ago and I can't focus on work, I can't sleep, I can't… You're in my head all the time…"

"Yeah," Jani whispered. "You're causing me that same problem."

She couldn't tell whether that pleased him or not. But she didn't really care. She was too lost in looking at him, at that impressive collection of features and those penetrating iridescent sea-green eyes.

And there was something undeniable and irresistible happening at that moment between them that she just couldn't fight.

So when he came slowly forward, Jani went slowly forward, too.

And when he kissed her, she was willing and eager to kiss him back because it felt like exactly what they were meant to do.…

There was an instant hunger and intensity to that kiss as their lips parted on contact and Gideon's tongue greeted hers.

Both of his hands came into her hair at once to cradle her head, bracing it against the kiss that Jani merely welcomed as she sent her own hands to press against the solid wall of his chest and massage just a little.

Just a little sensuously...

She knew that there was craziness to this, in this— she could feel it in the instant return of every bit of the desire she'd felt for him on Sunday night, in the tightening of her nipples, in their straining already for his touch.

But she suddenly didn't care. Maybe those three days apart had made her feel deprived and maybe deprivation had made her less cautious, but she was just so happy to be there with Gideon again, to have him kissing her the way he was, that that was all she cared about.

She vaguely recalled how she'd stopped him on Sunday night when she'd thought that if moments like this were all she could have with him, if she couldn't have anything more, she had to cut her losses and protect herself. But what she was thinking this time, as he plundered her mouth and she so happily gave way, was that her chances for romance once she was pregnant, once she was a single parent, were going to be greatly reduced. If not nil.

Whatever was happening between them right now could be her last chance for a long, *long* time.

And this was Gideon.

Her last time could be with him....

With this man whom she wanted more than any man ever...

It seemed crazy to deny herself that.

So she wasn't going to.

She was going to have him.

She just had to. Even if he was only kissing her so far, she just had to have more. She just had to have it all.…

She let her hands drop to his waist, to the hem of his sweater and she began to pull it upward, intent on taking it off of him.

But he instantly ended their kiss.

"Uh… Hi…" he said with a questioning glance down at what she was doing.

Jani smiled. Laughed. And said, "I thought maybe you…" She wanted to say: "should stay the night." But what she said was "…were hot."

"Oh, I'm hot all right," he said with a stirred-up sort of laugh that let her know it had nothing to do with temperature. "But wasn't it you who said we couldn't?"

"Maybe now we can…" Jani whispered with a tilt of her chin.

"Maybe?"

She merely grinned and kissed him, boldly sending her tongue on an expedition of its own.

But Gideon only indulged for a few minutes before he took her by the shoulders and pushed her out to arm's length.

"No maybes," he warned. "Either we can or we can't…"

"Well, I can," she said with a challenging tone that made him laugh before his brow crinkled into an almost pained sort of expression.

"Oh, believe me, I can, too. I just don't want you changing your mind at the last minute. Or hating me in the morning…"

"My mind won't change, and I can't imagine *ever* hating you...."

He studied her face, and Jani thought that a part of him was wondering if this was a trap of some kind.

But then he grinned and made a feral sort of groan as he pulled her to him to kiss her again. It was steamier even than before. Whatever minor inhibitions might have existed were gone and the only pause came when he finished the job she'd begun and tore off both his sweater and the T-shirt that was underneath it. But then he came right back to recapture her mouth with his.

Laying her palms on his bare skin opened the floodgates in Jani; she escaped from all thought to lose herself in what her wandering hands were discovering. In the feel of his naked chest, of his bulging biceps. In the pure breadth of his massive shoulders. In the heat of his broad back where the skin was smooth as her hands coursed all over it.

He had muscle everywhere there should have been muscle—hard and honed and strong. There was tautness where there should have been tautness, and more still when her hands explored his pectorals, causing his nipples to become almost as tight as hers were.

And hers were so, so tight, craving his touch...

He was taking his own sweet time, though, kissing her, kissing her, kissing her, holding her wrapped in arms that could have crushed her but merely enfolded her in the warmest embrace, leaving her breasts aching for some attention.

But still he didn't give it. Or at least not the way she expected.

Instead, just when she was considering placing one of his hands to one of her breasts herself, Gideon found the hem of her T-shirt, tugged it upward and then stopped kissing her to pull it over her head.

Which was when the unexpected came. Because while her wrists were caught in her sleeves, well over her head, he returned to kissing her—only what he was kissing now were her nipples. Kissing, nuzzling, then taking one fully into his mouth as he yanked her shirt completely off, threw it aside and clasped a hand to her other breast.

Jani couldn't keep from moaning softly, her arms drifting down to him again, to his back, just as he drew her breast farther in. And while his tongue traced the outer rim of her nipple, and then flicked at the crest, while his teeth tugged and nipped, his hand kneaded and caressed and lightly pinched, lighting glittering sparks inside her.

She was lying back on the sofa and she didn't even remember getting there. But Gideon was over her, on top of her, and the weight of him, what he was doing to her, only made her want him all the more. All the more urgently.

So urgently that even though it flitted through her mind that they could go upstairs, that possibly the lights should be turned off, there was nothing she could do but writhe as she experienced the wonders of what he was doing to her.

Then he reared up onto his knees, straddling her, and she saw some merit to the lights being on because she got to look at him. She got her first sight of his naked torso, and it was more amazing than it had been even to touch. Cut and carved, his body was a work of art.

A work of art that was still partially covered. She needed to remedy that.

Still drinking in the sight of him, she reached for the button keeping his waistband closed and unfastened it, not hesitating to lower the zipper that was nearly ready to burst, too.

Before she could go farther, he got up and turned off one of the end table lamps, leaving the room bathed in a more intimate light that Jani liked much better.

He took his wallet from the rear pocket of his jeans and pulled out a strip of condoms that gave Jani a moment of regret when she saw them.

But babies weren't what this was about, she reminded herself, shooing away even the thought to merely enjoy what was happening when Gideon peeled off his jeans and whatever was on underneath them.

Wow...

He was definitely a work of art. Everywhere. An example of the perfect male physique brought to grand and glorious life. And one glimpse of him in all his masculine beauty made Jani want him even more.

He returned to straddling her while he took away what remained of her clothes, too.

Having him study her the way she'd studied him was a little disconcerting until he groaned his approval, and then stretched out beside her.

He kissed her again, slowly but with such passion—passion intensified by what his big, strong hand was doing at her breasts at the same time—that needs she hadn't even known she had began to erupt inside of her.

She turned slightly toward him and insinuated one of her knees between his, bringing it upward, letting her thigh rest in the juncture of his legs as she reached for him, enclosing him in a grip that made him moan and tighten his hand at her breast.

Tongues went wild for a moment before he abandoned her mouth and kissed his way downward. Jani's spine arched involuntarily when he reached her breasts. Breasts that he delighted and delighted in, strumming a chord that seemed to run from there to the very core of her, and left her thinking she might peak before she should.

But just then he paused to put on protection. And when he returned, he rolled her to her back and came above her, between her welcoming legs, sliding into her in one smooth swing of his hips to hers.

Long and hard and sleek—he felt incredible inside of her, and together they were such a flawless fit that Jani had the fleeting thought that she'd been formed especially for him. And when he drew out, then in, then out and in again, she followed each ebb and flow to keep pace with a rhythm that came to her instinctively, naturally, as if that, too, was by some greater design that she'd just realized she belonged to.

Aware only of her body, and of his, of what they were doing together, she rode the waves, fingers clutching his back. It was heavenly torture when he drew away, and just plain heaven when he drove home again.

Growing, growing, growing—she could feel something that she couldn't possibly contain gaining power, a power like she'd never experienced. And then she lost the ability to breathe as it exploded and the most exquisite pleasure rippled all through her, holding her frozen and arched and silent until it began to pass and the tiniest of breathy moans escaped her throat as her lungs remembered to work.

Clinging to Gideon while her body barely began to come away from that splendor of all splendors, she felt him plunge even more deeply into her, more deeply than she thought possible. He pushed himself up on straight arms, bowed his spine and for one astonishing moment was rigid and still, reaching a height she felt reverberate from him into her in the superb shudder of his own release.

She lay beneath him, weak and spent and feeling oh-so-blissful. When the moment passed for him he eased himself down to her again kissing her in a way that seemed to seal them together completely. Then he held her tight and rolled so that she was suddenly on top, bodies still joined and melded together.

Her head went naturally to his chest and she turned to rest her cheek on the pillow of his pectoral, listening to the beat of his strong, strong heart while his arms wrapped her in more strength still.

"Wow…" he whispered, the exclamation more to himself than to her. "That was not like anything else—*ever*—for me," he added.

He sounded so shaken that it actually worried Jani. She tilted her head far back to look at him. "Bad?"

He laughed. "Bad? No! Why, was it bad for you?"

Now he was alarmed and that made Jani laugh just a little. "Oh, no," she said without the slightest uncertainty. "It was like nothing else—ever—for me, too. Do you think it's some weird fluke and neither of us has ever done it right before?"

That made him laugh again. "Maybe," he said. "I know I'm a little afraid nothing will ever live up to it."

She hadn't thought of that.…

"Maybe I should hang around and test it out," he suggested.

If he did, she wouldn't have just this one time, she'd have the whole night....

It was what she'd wanted to ask of him earlier.

But she concealed how happy that prospect made her by playing it cool. "Maybe you should... Purely for academic purposes."

He craned his head up and kissed the top of hers. "In the name of science," he said, pulsing inside of her.

"In the name of science," she confirmed.

He rolled them over again, this time to their sides, pinning her with her back to the rear cushions of the couch and her front to him.

"And what's a little sleep deprivation?" he asked, giving her tiny pecks of kisses.

"Sacrifices must be made," Jani answered.

Then he brought one hand to her breast, and flexed more deeply within her as he said, "Maybe we should make one more sacrifice before you show me the bedroom in this place..."

When she was about to say, *"Already?"* his mouth took hers again before she could, and talking became the last thing she cared about....

Chapter Ten

Jani might as well have stayed in bed with Gideon all day long on Thursday. It was what they'd both been tempted to do, and since she hadn't accomplished anything at work by the end of the afternoon, she was kicking herself for giving in to the call of duty.

As it was, after a night of barely dozing off between rounds of lovemaking, and making love again this morning, Gideon hadn't left her house until nine-thirty, and it had taken Jani until nearly eleven to get to her office. Where she hadn't been able to concentrate on anything because she'd only been able to think about Gideon. About the night they'd spent together.

And how she didn't think she could stand it if that one night was all they had...

She'd reminded herself a hundred times today that sleeping with Gideon was supposed to have been a sort of last hurrah for her. One final indulgence before she got pregnant and became a single parent. A nice memory to carry with her.

But that was *all* it was supposed to have been.

And yet today she just couldn't accept it for that.

Her feelings for Gideon wouldn't *let* her accept it for that.

She didn't want to put a name to what she was feeling but deep down she knew what it was. And she knew it was stronger than even what she'd felt for Reggie.

She wanted the man.

She wanted the man and everything else, too—a long life with him, kids with him, going to bed with him every night, seeing his face first thing every morning. She wanted him by her side through the highs and the lows, she wanted to grow old with him.

She wanted it all with him so much that she was dreading the appointment she'd made for Friday to go through the donor profile notebook at the doctor's office again.

Because she knew that there wasn't anyone in it whom she wanted to father her baby. She wanted the father to be Gideon. Now that she'd met Gideon, now that she had feelings for him, it made it very difficult to go on with her plans for artificial insemination and single parenthood.

There was a voice in the back of her mind shouting that she was about to step into the pitfall she'd sworn to avoid. That having a child on her own was the solution to the problems that came with hanging her hopes on a man, a relationship. Her way to make sure she had the family she wanted while she still could.

But that voice wasn't as loud as the other thoughts that were running through her mind.

She just couldn't help thinking that Gideon was so much better a man than Reggie had been. He was honest and upstanding. He had integrity, loyalty, values, a strong sense of himself and his responsibilities. He was intelligent and ambitious and true to his convictions.

And if all of that wasn't enough, he was great company, and amazingly good-looking, and she'd never clicked with anyone the way she did with him—out of bed and—now she knew—in bed, too.

They were just perfect together—that was what the louder voice in her head kept telling her. He was exactly whom she wanted to have kids with, and suddenly the secret wish that there might be a chance with him had leaped to the surface and taken over as an undeniable need to see if she couldn't make it work with Gideon.

Am I just hopelessly stupid and naive? she asked herself as she sat at her desk. *First Reggie with the gambling problem and now Gideon who hates Camdens and doesn't want kids.*

She had to admit that even entertaining the idea that she could make things work with Gideon seemed hopelessly stupid and naive. Ridiculously, unrealistically stupid and naive, in fact.

Because wanting someone to be different, hoping they could be different, trying to urge and push and cajole them to be different the way she had with Reggie, didn't make them different. She'd learned that. Over and over again.

And yet…

There was still that louder voice also telling her that Reggie's need to gamble was an addiction. A compulsion. A deeply rooted part of his personality, his character, his makeup.

But that wasn't what was going on with Gideon.

His resentment of the Camdens was definitely deeply rooted. But she didn't believe that it was an intrinsic part of his personality or his character. His family's hatred of the Camdens and what they had suffered because of H.J. was just something that had had a strong influence on Gideon.

But now maybe so had she.

Not only had she been on a mission to make amends with the community center, but Gideon had said himself when he'd come over last night that clearing his great-grandfather's name in that newspaper article had lifted a weight from his shoulders. He'd *thanked* her.

That might not be a complete pardon for what H.J. had done. But at least she'd begun the healing process for the injuries that were standing in the way of having a future with Gideon.

That was very different than Reggie's gambling addiction, which couldn't be fixed.

And although it worried her that she could be wrong, it also seemed as if Gideon's anti-kid policy might be curable, too.

He'd been badly hurt by losing that little girl he'd thought of as his own. And his response was to swear he'd never let himself be vulnerable again, that he'd stay childless to protect himself.

But a man like Gideon—who had the capability of loving a child that much, who could be such a great dad, who had said himself that he'd genuinely liked being a parent—was precisely the type of man who *should* have kids. And Jani thought it was possible that he would eventually come to that conclusion. That once this particular wound had healed and scarred over, he might even *want* to try parenthood again.

She honestly thought it was just a matter of time.

Time that she didn't have to spend…

But maybe if she could talk to him, reason with him—

Fix him?

Okay, the voice of caution was a little louder now. Probably because yes, what she was considering did constitute trying to fix something the way she'd mistakenly thought she could fix Reggie. But it wasn't Gideon she was trying to fix—there wasn't a single thing wrong with him. She needed to fix the problems that stood in the way of having what she wanted with him.

And she knew that if she didn't make some effort to solve these particular problems, she wasn't going to get what she wanted. She was just going to end up at the doctor's office again tomorrow, looking through profiles of strangers to father the baby she would have without Gideon.

And raise without Gideon…

So she thought that she had to at least go to him and lay her cards on the table.

She had to take the risk.

She had to because she could see so clearly what a great life she and Gideon could have together.

Because she could see so clearly what beautiful kids they could have together.

Because *those* were the kids she wanted and the way she wanted to have them—sharing the whole experience with Gideon.

And because she couldn't let it all slip through her fingers without taking that one last chance.

* * *

"Jani?"

Gideon was stunned to arrive at his loft at eight o'clock Thursday evening and find Jani sitting on the corridor floor outside his door, sound asleep.

Apparently his voice wasn't loud enough to wake her because she was still out like a light.

For a moment he stood there above her, looking at her.

God, she was beautiful!

Dark hair fell around the alabaster skin of a face that a master's hand could have sculpted. She'd taken off her coat, and the navy blue knit dress she was wearing hugged every curve of the tight little body that he just wanted his hands all over again the way they'd been last night and this morning. Her coat was draped across her lap but her legs were still visible, and there was no doubt about it—they were the best legs he'd ever seen, long and lean and shapely, with thin ankles above the four-inch heels that no woman he'd ever known could wear as well as Jani.

And after a day spent in utter confusion in regards to her, he just wanted to scoop her up, take her to his bed and let tonight be a repeat of last night.

But the confusion had been just torturous enough to keep him from doing that. Instead he hunkered down on his heels beside her, brushed her hair away from her delicately featured face and said again, more loudly, more firmly, "Jani?"

It registered this time. She jolted slightly, blinked her eyes and sat up straight.

Gideon could tell by the disorientation in her gorgeous blue eyes that she didn't at first know where she was. But after a moment of glancing around, her gaze ended up on him and she smiled that lazy smile he'd seen a couple of times last night—that lazy smile that was a vision of sensuality and enough to turn him on all by itself.

But he fought the reaction and merely gave her a tentative smile in return. "Hi," he said in a tone that asked why she was there even though he was so glad she was he didn't care why.

"What time is it?" she asked.

"Eight."

"You worked late…"

"I got a late start," he reminded her, unable to keep from grinning at the thought of why he hadn't made it to the office when he should have.

"Me, too," she said with the same kind of grin. "But I was so scattered that I couldn't get anything done anyway, so I left when I usually do."

Gideon stood back up, bent over to take her hand and helped her to her feet.

He tried not to notice how soft her skin was, how small and fragile her hand felt in his, how much he just liked touching her. But he couldn't help it.

As soon as she was steady on her high heels, he let go of her and turned to unlock the door.

"Scattered, huh?" he said as he ushered her into the loft.

Even though he'd spent the day conflicted over what they'd already done, even though he knew he shouldn't do it again, he was already trying to find a way to give himself permission for yet another night with her.

But he wasn't so sure that was a possibility when she

said, "I just couldn't get into work. I did a lot of thinking—about you and me—and I had to talk to you."

He took off his overcoat and tossed it across the back of one of the side chairs. Then he hooked a leg over the corner of the sofa back and propped himself there. It was intended to appear nonchalant but the truth was he was anchoring himself to keep from going to Jani and kissing her.

She was still standing there, barely inside the door he'd closed behind them. He could see that she was keeping her distance and he didn't think that boded well for anything.

"Okay. What do you want to talk about?" he asked.

"I…" she began, but she stalled, seemed to struggle for the words, then started again, "Last night was a big deal for me. Everything with you has been a big deal for me."

Gideon wasn't sure what that meant. But then she went on to tell him. To talk about having feelings for him. About wanting to have a future with him. About wanting his babies…

"I know how you feel," she said when she'd gotten all of it out. Gideon figured that his expression probably showed the alarm that was going off inside him.

But still she took one step closer, as if that didn't scare her off.

"I know you might think of yourself as a traitor for having anything to do with me or any Camden," she went on. "And I know the agony of losing that little girl you thought of as your daughter is still fresh enough for you to recoil at the thought of having kids. But if you could just get past it all and focus on what we have together… I just think that it's too good to let anything stand in our way."

"Jani—"

"I know," she cut him short. "It was kind of off-putting for you to wake up this morning *in bed with a Camden*—"

He'd said it jokingly. But the joke hadn't completely concealed that there had been a certain amount of guilt, too.

"—I know that this whole thing is complicated," she continued. "I know the last thing you ever thought you'd do is become part of the Camden family. The last thing you ever wanted to do. And I can't say I'll ever renounce being a Camden, turn my back on my family or anything like that. I know what I'm asking is for you to—"

"Come over to the dark side?" he said facetiously.

Jani shrugged. "Yes. I know that's how you've always thought of us. But you've seen for yourself who we are now. You know we hate what happened to your family because of H.J., and that we just want to make it up to you. That we're trying—GiGi even wants me to offer the Thatcher Group the chance to build every Camden Superstore from here on, if you're interested… Not that that's what I came to talk to you about tonight."

"You came to talk to me about things bigger than you think," he said. Because while he felt an urge to just take her in his arms and say yes to anything she wanted, there was a whole lot of other baggage dragging him down and stopping him.

"I don't believe that," she insisted. "No Camdens, no kids—I know you think those are some kind of carved-in-stone, irrefutable laws that there's no turning back from. But I think they're really something else. I think they're just your response to wounds—old ones and new ones. Wounds that can be healed. You said last night that you felt like a weight had been lifted off you because I set the record straight about your great-grandfather—that says to me that you're beginning to heal. Isn't that possible?"

"It helped," Gideon acknowledged because he wasn't going to withhold credit where credit was due.

"And now there will be the community center in Franklin Thatcher's name. Instead of looking at yourself as some kind of traitor, couldn't you look at it all and know that you're the Thatcher who got restitution for your family—"

"Restitution?" Gideon couldn't help scoffing at that. "Nothing that happens now makes anything up to my great-grandfather or my grandfather or my father. They still lived the lives they led because of what happened, Jani—"

"But do you owe them *your* life because of it? Can't you put the past behind you?"

"I don't know about that," Gideon answered her honestly.

"Or maybe you could just be the one to forgive us on their behalf," she suggested. "Maybe Franklin Thatcher didn't come to it, maybe your grandfather and your father didn't come to it, but that doesn't mean you can't come to it…"

"The wrongs just aren't mine to forgive," he said because that was what he believed.

"But you *could* forgive us for what you suffered in the fallout. You *could* choose to put the past behind *you,*" she repeated so earnestly it nearly broke his heart.

But it didn't change things. Even if she'd taken some

of the heaviness out of the old baggage, he still couldn't imagine himself going over so completely to the enemy camp. Plus there was the even bigger issue of kids.

And that issue was all his own.

As if she could read his mind, she said, "And when it comes to kids... I know—I *saw* in you—how awful it was for you to lose that little girl. I know it's still fresh to you—if you've only been in this place for six months, it couldn't have been long before that—"

"It's been about a year."

"Still, that's not that long to get completely over something so painful, and I understand that you want to make sure you never go through anything like that again. But—"

She went on to talk about how good he was with kids, about a whole lot of other things that he just didn't hear because he was suddenly lost in thoughts of Jillie, in recalling the pain, the frustration, the utter helplessness he'd felt when there was nothing he could do to stop Shelly from taking her away.

He was thinking about the empty days and nights after that.

About all the times when he'd thought he could still hear Jillie playing in the next room only to feel like he'd been hit with a baseball bat when he realized that it wasn't true.

About the worry he still had every day if she was well or being taken care of the way she should be, if she was happy or sad. If she cried for him or needed him, and he wasn't there...

While Jani was talking about how she knew he would want kids again, he was thinking about having a child who was half Camden. About how even though that child might be half his—unlike Jillie—the power and money and prestige and status of the Camdens could give Jani the upper hand and almost as strong a position from which to play keep-away with a child as Shelly had had with Jillie.

And one way or another, he'd still lose.

It just wasn't a position he could put himself in again...

"Stop, Jani. Stop," he heard himself say before she went on any longer.

"No, don't tell me to stop," she protested.

"If you think this isn't ripping me apart, you're wrong," he heard himself say, the emotions hitting the surface and sending the words out before he even knew he was going to say them. "But I can't, Jani. Even if we could take away my family's history with the Camdens, I won't ever—*ever*—have kids. And that's a dealbreaker for you."

She did stop then. Totally. She just stood there looking at him. She was so beautiful he could hardly believe it, and he could see that he'd crushed her. But that she was trying not to show it.

"Am I just being a dumb girl and thinking that there was more here than there actually was?" she asked.

Now he thought that he knew what she was thinking.

"No," he said without hesitation. "There's plenty here. And I didn't sleep with you to get even or something truly lowlife like that. I have the same feelings about you that you said you have about me—I'm...I'm crazy about you. And even right at this minute keeping my hands off you is the hardest thing I've ever had to do. But—"

"But nothing. Everything else is nothing compared to that," she insisted.

"Maybe it's nothing to you, but it's not nothing to me," he said, shaking his head. His voice was a deep, sad rumble but that was the only way he could get the words out. "No Camdens. No kids. You were right about both of those things. Especially about the no kids part—"

"Especially no Camden kids," she said, her voice cracking.

Gideon didn't respond because yes, at that moment he really was thinking *especially no Camden kids*. But to confirm it was a blow he didn't want to strike.

Even so he saw her eyes well up. But she didn't let the tears fall. She was still facing him with her head high, her back straight, and he had the impression that maintaining her composure was taking all the strength she could muster.

He didn't know what else to say so he seized the subject of business and said, "I'll understand if you want to pull the funding for the community center. And I'll return your grandmother's check."

She shook her head. "That's separate from any of this. It's what we all want to do. For Franklin Thatcher. For Lakeview." She swallowed hard. "I'll just arrange for you to work from here on with someone else in the family. Cade, maybe…"

She'd been holding her coat in front of her and now she put it on, not looking at him while she did.

Then she turned toward the door and paused.

With her hand on the knob, facing away from him, she said with the tears in her throat now, "It's a mistake, you know? To wrap yourself in hurts and wounds and grudges and all of that? It might keep you safe but it isn't going to be there to open packages with you on Christmas mornings, or to draw you silly pictures to put on the fridge, or to fill your life. I'll risk that there might be a downside in order to have the up…" She opened his door, walked out and closed it behind her.

Leaving Gideon with a wave of pain that reminded him much too much of the day he watched Shelly take Jillie away…

Chapter Eleven

"So…Monday is my awards lunch—I just set it up to have barbecue brought in for everybody," Gideon informed Jack when he stopped by his friend's office on his way out for the weekend.

"Your awards lunch?" Jack repeated, confused.

"Yeah, you know, for being the world's biggest jerk this whole last week."

Jack laughed. Gideon appreciated that his friend could still find some humor in the way things had been around the office since Jani had left his apartment eight days ago. Gideon hadn't intended to take out his rotten mood on anyone else but it had still spilled over into work and he wouldn't have blamed Jack—or anyone else at the Thatcher Group—for telling him where he could stick his consolation lunch.

"Are you doing any better?" There was sympathy in Jack's question.

"No. But that tirade I threw over files that weren't lost because they were right there on my desk, in front of my face, was enough. I just sent out a blanket apology email to everybody with the invitation to lunch, and I swear when I come back on Monday, I'll keep my lousy frame of mind to myself."

"Either that or you might have a mutiny on your hands," Jack joked.

"I know, I know—I've been an ass."

"Remind you of any other time?" Jack asked, grabbing his coat and joining Gideon to head out of the building for the weekend.

"Yeah, I'm also aware that I was not easy to work with when Shelly took Jillie away."

"I have to drive to Colorado Springs to pick up Sammy or I'd take you to a bar, buy you a few drinks and then tell you what I think instead of just crying in my beer right along with you—like I did last weekend. But I can't draw this out so I'm going to cut to the chase. When Shelly went nuts enough to opt out of your marriage and take Jillie away, you didn't have any choice. But now? You did this to yourself, buddy. You could have Jani but *you* turned *her* down. And even though I know your reasons, it seems to me you ought to take another look at them because in order to avoid misery, you've walked headlong into it."

Gideon would have liked to argue, but not only did his friend have to go, Jack was right. "Yeah. I know that, too," he grumbled.

"No Camdens. No kids. Those are the rules. I got it. But for what it's worth? Let go of 'em both and seize the day—that's my advice."

"Advice you'd be able to take?"

Jack laughed. "Yeah, I'm a little too raw to take it right now. But I'm hoping for the best—that I'll get over this and go on to something better, something that *does* work. Maybe that's what you've stumbled into. And all you have to do is say yes to it."

Gideon didn't respond in any way to that. Instead he said, "Drive safe to the Springs—in case of mutiny I might need you to defend me."

"I've always got your back," Jack assured before they went their separate ways.

It was Friday night. The second Friday night since he'd parted with Jani. At least last Friday night he and Jack had gone out, and Jack had commiserated with him. Then on Saturday and Sunday they'd played racquetball and basketball and indoor tennis. They'd done more bar-hopping on Saturday night, and taken in a movie on Sunday night—all to exhaust and distract him for the weekend.

But this weekend Jack had his son.

Gideon was on his own.

After what easily qualified as one of the worst weeks of his life, he was now facing two days with nothing but his own company and unbearable bad spirits.

That was what Gideon was thinking as he got behind the wheel of his car and started the engine.

Two days with nothing but his own sad company. Or he could be going home, showering, taking Jani to dinner and spending from now until Monday morning with her.

Hell, he could be going home to her right now....

Except that she was a Camden.

Who wanted kids.

Which meant that having her had to include having

kids. And having kids could put him in line for losing kids. Kids who would be half Camdens and would irrefutably connect him to the Camden clan for the rest of his life. Birthdays, holidays, parties, cookouts, celebrations, Sunday dinners—for every bit of it, he'd be with the Camdens...

With the Camdens...

He knew he was in a bad way when he couldn't even muster up any old resentment at the thought of the entire Camden clan. When the thought of another Sunday dinner at Georgianna Camden's house even had some appeal.

Maybe he really *was* a traitor, he thought as he pulled into the parking garage below his apartment building and found his spot.

Certainly at that moment loyalty was cold comfort...

He got out of his car and trudged to the elevator, having the same ridiculous sense of hope that he'd had every time he'd made that walk since a week ago Thursday. The stupid, self-torturing hope that this time would be like that time—that he'd ride the elevator up to his floor, the doors would open, and there Jani would be again, waiting for him.

But tonight—like every other night—the corridor was empty when he got there. Of course, he knew it would be.

Still, though, disappointment fell over him like a deflated parachute as he unlocked the door to the loft.

And Jack's words seemed to echo from the sterile interior as he stepped inside.

You did this to yourself....

In order to avoid misery you walked headlong into it....

Jack had also told him to take another look at his reasons for turning Jani down.

He just didn't want to. The more he thought about everything—and that was all he'd done the past eight days when he wasn't biting somebody's head off—the weaker his reasons seemed to get.

He actually laughed mirthlessly at that thought when he threw his coat across a bar stool.

"Don't look at the justification for something because that justification can't hold up?" he said out loud.

But his reasons for turning Jani down *did* hold up. They were valid. They hadn't gotten weaker.

It was just that Jani had been added to the equation.

His feelings for Jani had been added to the equation.

And that had altered things.

That had made his reasons *seem* weaker by comparison because his feelings for her were just bigger and stronger.

Okay, he hadn't admitted it to himself until that moment, but now, as he went into the bedroom to get out of his work clothes, he suddenly faced facts.

The size and strength of what he felt for Jani made it impossible for him not to question himself—and this choice he'd made that was killing him.

He yanked the knot out of his tie and pulled the strip of Italian silk from around his neck. As he went to the tie rack attached to the side of his dresser, he caught sight of a photograph he kept on the bureau.

The picture was of his great-grandfather, his grandfather and his father at barely twenty-one, all of them standing on the sidewalk in front of the bar that had been the center of the Thatchers' lives.

He picked up the framed photograph and took it with

him to sit on the edge of his bed and stare at it, remembering...

In the picture his father and his work-worn grandfather smiled for the camera, but his great-grandfather was somber. Gideon knew that by the time the picture had been taken, Franklin Thatcher had lost all hope of ever reclaiming his reputation or any of the life he'd had taken away from him in the Lakeview debacle.

"I'm doing what I can, Pops," he said to that image of his great-grandfather. "I'm redeveloping Lakeview the way you wanted. There will be a community center in your honor—the Franklin Thatcher Community Center. And your name is being cleared in a newspaper article—I know you would have liked that."

He genuinely would have, Gideon thought. It might be decades late, but he knew that it would have been a huge deal to the old, old man he'd known when he was a child. It would have been a huge deal to have this kind of public acknowledgment.

And even coming late, it was still something.

But the question in Gideon's mind was: Did all he'd done, all he was doing, earn him something in return?

A pat on the back. His great-grandfather's appreciation. Pride in him from his family—sure, it would have earned him those things.

But a free path to the Camdens? A charge to *go get her*?

Never. There wasn't a doubt in Gideon's mind about that—he'd heard enough from all three previous generations to know what they all thought of the Camdens. How they felt about them. To his great-grandfather, his grandfather, his father, the Camdens would have remained the dirty low-down dogs who destroyed the Thatchers.

But thinking of Jani as a dirty low-down dog was just ridiculous.

In fact, he even found it a little difficult to think of the rest of the Camdens he'd met as that.

They just weren't.

But then, he wasn't his father or his grandfather or his great-grandfather, either...

Then it struck him.

He was a different man than those who had come before him. He'd worked *not* to end up in that bar, to rise above what the past had left the Thatchers with. He'd learned from their mistakes. He was a new breed of Thatcher.

And if he was a new breed of Thatcher, couldn't he accept that Jani's family was a new breed of Camdens? That they might all be like Jani—decent, honest, honorable people?

That *was* what they were known for now, despite some of the stigma that remained from their past.

So should they be held responsible for what was done by earlier generations?

He didn't feel responsible for anything done by the generations before him, he realized. And like what he was doing in Lakeview, the Camdens were trying to make up for the past despite the fact that they'd had no hand in it.

In one way or another, weren't they all pretty much working for the same thing? he asked himself. To set old wrongs right?

They were.

And maybe it was part of making things right again

to do what Jani had suggested he do—put the past behind him. Certainly it didn't seem fair to him, at that moment, to be forever tied to those old wrongs.

But there was still the kid issue.

Jani thought that he would eventually get over his problems with that. That time would heal the wound of losing Jillie and he'd want kids again.

It wasn't something he'd let himself think about since deciding to take a no-kids route. But difficult as it was, he forced himself to consider her perspective as he went on sitting on the edge of his bed.

Okay, yeah, he really had loved being a dad.

And yes, he really did like kids.

And a kid with Jani?

He closed his eyes. He took a deep breath.

Yeah, he could see himself wanting a kid with Jani.

God help him, he could actually see himself wanting that a lot.

Suddenly the feeling was much bigger and stronger than the suffering he'd gone through over losing Jillie...

He hadn't thought that anything could ever diminish that pain.

But at that moment he knew that not only did he want Jani with every fiber of his being, in every way, every minute of every day and night, he also knew that he didn't want her to have a baby the way she planned to. Or worse yet, with another man. He didn't want her to have a baby without him....

It terrified him. But yes, deep down there was the desire to be the father of her baby.

A Camden baby.

One who could bring a wall of Camden power between him and that child if things ever ended with Jani...

He wavered.

But some people do stay together...

The thought came out of nowhere and he didn't shoo it away. He felt as if his life was hanging in the balance and he *needed* to entertain it to survive.

But it was true—some people *did* stay together. They had kids and raised them together. They actually did what Jani had said she wanted—they had an entire future together, they grew old together, they enjoyed their grown kids and their grandkids and their great-grandkids. Together.

And if he could have that?

It wasn't a big leap to knowing that yes, if he could have Jani, if he could have a family with her that he never, ever lost, then that was exactly what he wanted.

Even if she *was* a Camden.

He wanted it so much—he wanted her so much—that he knew he had to give in.

Because regardless of who she was, regardless of what he'd thought since Shelly had left him, when it came to Jani, when it meant not having her, he just couldn't keep an old grudge alive another day, and he couldn't play it safe.

He sat up straight and took the photograph from where he'd set it on the mattress beside him, looking at it again.

"I'm sorry," he said to the men in the picture, to the family that had come before him and suffered because of Jani's ancestors. "But I have to have her." He shook his head again, resolved. "I *have* to have her..."

* * *

"Just dinner, Jani. Lindie and I will pick you up, we'll go somewhere quiet and nice, we can talk about him or not talk about him, we can do anything you want…"

Jani appreciated what her cousins were offering but it had been a long and awful week after a long and awful weekend last weekend. She'd spent most of the past eight days talking about Gideon. She knew that all of her family had to be sick of hearing about him. She was actually sick of talking about him.

"Thanks, but I've already showered and washed my hair," she told Livi. "I'm in pajama pants and a T-shirt and slippers, I'm just going to go to bed early and try to catch up on some sleep." Which she'd lost a lot of…

"You're not going to sleep at seven o'clock," her cousin insisted. "What if we come there, order in, maybe watch some tear-jerker movie—"

She didn't think she could stand to cry more tears.

"—or a comedy," Livi amended, realizing her mistake.

But there was nothing that could make her laugh, either.

"No, really Liv, it's okay," Jani said wearily. "Shoe shopping with you guys tomorrow will be good— maybe we can have dinner after that. But for tonight I'm just going to fix myself a sandwich and go to bed early."

"How about a sleepover?" her cousin said as if she'd just had a brainstorm.

"Liv! No! Really, I'm okay. But I have to go—somebody is at my door."

"Keep me on the line while you see who it is, just in case," Livi ordered.

"Okay." Jani understood that her family worried

about her after what had happened over Reggie. She took the phone with her as she went to peer through the peephole of her front door.

"It's him!" she whispered when she saw Gideon standing in the light of her front porch.

"Him Gideon? Or him someone scary?" Livi asked, on the verge of alarm.

"It's Gideon."

"Do you want to see him?"

More than she wanted air to breathe.

But what she said was, "I guess. Maybe he's here about something to do with the community center or that article or something." She didn't want to get her hopes up that he was there for a better reason.

"Do you want me to come over so you don't have to be alone with him?"

Being alone with Gideon was something else she wanted desperately. She just wasn't sure she could bear it if he was only there about business.

But he *was* there. And there was nothing that could keep her from finding out why, even if it meant it was strictly business and hurt her all over again the way his rejection had hurt her last week.

"No, don't come over. There's nothing to be afraid of—he's not one of Reggie's bookie's thugs."

"Call me when he leaves, then," Livi commanded.

Jani hung up and set the phone on the entry table. As she opened the door, her heart beat so hard and fast she wondered if it was going to beat right out of her chest.

But she put some effort into only showing a questioning surprise at the fact that Gideon was her visitor.

"Hi," he said as if he knew that sounded feeble.

"Hi," she parroted.

"Are you busy? Going out? Do you have company?"

"No, none of the above," she said simply.

"Then can we talk?"

She considered asking what he wanted to talk about so she had some idea of what to expect. But it wasn't as if she was going to turn him away regardless, so she merely stepped back and said, "Sure. Come in."

He did, looking ragged around the edges despite the fact that he was clean-shaven and smelled of soap and cologne, telling her that he was fresh from a shower, too. And though he showed signs that he'd had a week as difficult as Jani's, he still looked bad-boy delicious in jeans and a black turtleneck sweater with his hair combed carelessly and the collar of his coat turned up to his chiseled jawline.

But Jani tried not to revel in the sight of him too much.

She also tried not to let her hopes get too high that he was there for a reason better than business…

Closing the door behind him once he was in her entryway, she said, "Would you like to sit down?"

He didn't answer, he merely went into the living room. And he didn't sit. He stood in the center of the room, his hands in the pockets of the long overcoat that flapped open down the front.

Jani joined him but she didn't sit, either. She just propped one shin on the arm of the first easy chair she came to, keeping her distance.

"Am I too late?" he asked out of the blue.

Jani's head had been so muddled since she'd left his loft over a week ago that for a moment she thought she might have missed something—an invitation, maybe?

She just wasn't sure what he was talking about. "Are you too late for what?"

"You know—the baby-making. Have you gone through with the artificial insemination?"

For some reason that seemed too personal to talk about to him now so her voice was quiet when she said a simple, "No, not yet."

What she didn't tell him was that she could have begun the process but had been so upset about him that she'd opted to let another month go by, even though she knew she shouldn't waste more of her dwindling time. But she just hadn't been able to choose someone other than Gideon to be the father of her baby. And she definitely hadn't thought it was time to attempt to conceive when she was so horribly, hideously unhappy.

"Then you're not pregnant—great!" he said on a sigh of what sounded like relief.

He was so glad about that that it almost made her cry—for the millionth time since she'd last seen him. Was fate just having a laugh at her expense by making her fall as hard as she had for someone *that* anti-baby? And now what? Had he decided he could overlook her being a Camden if only she could give up having kids?

Don't ask me to make that choice....

"No, I'm not pregnant," she confirmed cautiously.

"Then I'm not too late."

"Because you came to stop me?" she asked, still fearing the worst.

"I came to tell you that I don't want to spend another week—another minute—like the last week. Without you…" he said.

He went on to tell her how bad the week had actually been for him—reflecting back to her the same kind of gloom and despair and awful mood she'd suffered.

Then he talked about today, tonight, and how he'd finally sorted through the things that were keeping them apart.

"It's complicated, Jani," he said. "But you were right about a lot of things and I realized that if I let myself be tied forever to the past I'd be robbing myself of having the future that I want with you—"

"A future with a Camden? Didn't you say that would mean crossing over to the dark side?"

"Yeah, a little," he said without hesitation. "I can't say that I don't feel some guilt for aligning myself with a Camden. Some disloyalty. I can't say that there might not be times when I look around at all your family has and think that some of it came at the expense of my family. But what's between you and me…" He shook his head in awe. "It *is* too good to let anything stand in our way. No matter what happened before between H.J. and my great-grandfather, no matter how that rippled through the other generations, right now, today, I'm in love with you, Jani. I'm more in love with you than I've ever been with anyone. And I can't go through another day of my life without you."

Jani studied him, touched and overjoyed and thrilled because yes, those *were* some of the words she'd wanted desperately to hear.

But there was still the baby issue and she was also afraid of what might come next. Did he hope she would trade her goal of having a baby for the love he was offering her?

"I want kids…" she whispered, opening that door with dread.

Gideon came to stand in front of her, taking her upper arms in his strong hands and bringing her to her feet so he could pull her closer.

"I know," he said. "And I also can't tell you that that doesn't scare me. But I love you," he said again. "I love you so much it hurts. And when I think about you having a kid, I can't stand the thought of it being any kid but mine."

"That isn't the same as wanting kids," Jani pointed out.

"Then I'm saying it wrong because yeah, there's that, too," he admitted. "I want kids with you. You were right, I did like being a dad and when I thought about it I could see your point—I could see maybe someday wanting that again—"

"But with me, *someday* needs to be today."

"I know." He laughed at her nervousness. "That's why I want you to marry me. Fast!" he said, lightening the tone. "Because I really do want us to have the whole package. I want us to lock this thing down tight and never let go." He sobered and she saw his own concerns come to the surface before he said with his heart on his sleeve, "Just tell me we won't ever let go."

She knew that that was what he was really worried about and, given his history, she understood that.

"Letting go of you isn't something I ever want to do," she said softly, sincerely.

"I hope you mean that. I hope you'll always mean that," he whispered.

Jani saw his raw vulnerability and knew that nothing could fully reassure him, that only time would prove what she knew in her heart—that they would be together forever.

But she reached a palm to the side of his face, stood on tiptoe and kissed him before she said, "I love you, Gideon. More than I've ever loved anyone. More than I knew I *could* love anyone. I love you the way I imagine that people who spend their whole lives together must love each other. If it will make you feel better, I'll sign a custody agreement before we even have kids because I'm so sure that it will never have to be used—"

"Instead of a prenup we'll have a prenatal—that gives a whole new meaning to the word doesn't it?" he joked.

"Still—"

"I'll think about it," he said, smiling that smile that had been so slow in coming when they'd first met, that smile that sent a warm rush through her whenever she saw it. "Just say you'll marry me and the rest—"

"I will," Jani answered with a laugh of her own, blinking back happy tears now that it was sinking in that she was getting exactly what she wanted.

Gideon's smile grew into a grin. He stared into her eyes as if he needed a moment to accept that he was getting what he wanted, too. Then he kissed her again—so firmly it staked his claim on her—before he said hopefully, "Maybe we can put my great-grandfather's name on something better than a community center—like his first great-great-grandson?"

"Or his first great-great-granddaughter—we could call her Frankie."

"I like that, too," Gideon said with a laugh.

Then he kissed her once more, so passionately now that she knew that this was not the night she was going to catch up on her sleep.

When he ended that kiss, rather than whisking her to

the bedroom the way she thought he might, he instead held her so close that her head became a shelf for his chin and his arms wrapped around her like a vise, as if to convince himself that all this was genuinely real.

But they couldn't stay in each other's arms for long without things heating up, so after a few moments he whispered a sexy whisper into her hair. "With any luck maybe we can get great-great-grand Frankie started tonight."

Jani laughed. "It *is* prime time. I just couldn't go through with anything that might have given me a baby that wasn't yours...."

He kissed the top of her head poignantly but camouflaged that poignancy by saying, "Then let's see if we can't get this rolling."

He let go of her to take her hand and lead her out of the living room to the bedroom.

The bedroom where Jani suddenly felt sure they actually would make a baby. Maybe even bab*ies*.

Because she loved him too much to believe that anything would keep her from having what she wanted now that she had him.

This man she loved almost more than she could bear.

* * * * *

SPECIAL EXCERPT FROM

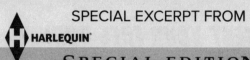

HARLEQUIN®

SPECIAL EDITION

USA TODAY *bestselling author Allison Leigh*
brings us a sneak peek of A WEAVER VOW,
a new tale of love, loss and second chances in her
RETURN TO THE DOUBLE-C *miniseries for*
Harlequin® Special Edition®.

***

Murphy, please don't get into more trouble.

Whatever had made her think she could be a better parent to Murphy than his other options? He needed a man around, not just a woman he could barely tolerate.

He needed his father.

And now all they had was each other.

Isabella Lockhart couldn't bear to think about it.

"It was an accident!" Murphy yelled. "Dude! That's my bat. You can't just take my bat!"

"I just did, *dude*," the man returned flatly. He closed his hand over Murphy's thin shoulder and forcibly moved him away from Isabella.

Isabella rounded on the man, gaping at him. He was wearing a faded brown ball cap and aviator sunglasses that hid his eyes. "Take your hand off him! Who do you think you are?"

"The man your boy decided to aim at with his blasted baseball." His jaw was sharp and shadowed by brown stubble and his lips were thinned.

"I did not!" Murphy screamed right into Isabella's ear.

She winced, then pointed. "Go sit down."

She drew in a calming breath and turned her head into the breeze that she'd begun to suspect never died here in Weaver, Wyoming, before facing the man again. "I'm Isabella Lockhart," she began.

"I know who you are."

She'd been in Weaver only a few weeks, but it really was a small town if people she'd never met already knew who she was.

"I'm sure we can resolve whatever's happened here, Mr. uh—?"

"Erik Clay."

Focusing on the woman in front of him was a lot safer than focusing on the skinny black-haired hellion sprawled on Ruby's bench.

She tucked her white-blond hair behind her ear with a visibly shaking hand. Bleached blond, he figured, considering the eyes that she turned toward the back of his truck were such a dark brown they were nearly black.

Even angry as he was, he wasn't blind to the whole effect. Weaver's newcomer was a serious looker.

***

Don't miss A WEAVER VOW
by USA TODAY *bestselling author Allison Leigh.*

Available in May 2013 from
Harlequin® Special Edition® wherever books are sold.

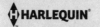

EXPECTING FORTUNE'S HEIR
by Cindy Kirk

Shane Fortune is accustomed to women using his
family for money, so when the cute and spunky
Lia Serrano tells him that she is pregnant with his
baby after a one-night stand, he is seriously skeptical.
But after spending more time together, he can't help
but hope the baby is truly his....

Look for the next book in
The Fortunes of Texas:
Southern Invasion

Available in May from Harlequin Special Edition,
wherever books are sold.